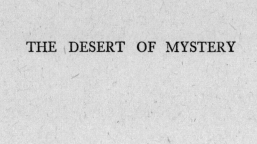

THE DESERT OF MYSTERY

THE DESERT OF MYSTERY

by

VICTOR APPLETON

THE CHILDREN'S PRESS
LONDON AND GLASGOW

First Printed in this Edition 1953

CONTENTS

CHAP.		PAGE
I	A COWARDLY ATTACK	11
II	TO THE RESCUE	19
III	THE MASTER OF CAMELS	27
IV	THE CITY OF BRASS	37
V	A DANGEROUS UNDERTAKING	45
VI	A GLIMPSE OF OLD ENEMIES	49
VII	THE FIGHT FOR MASTERY	57
VIII	INTO THE DESERT WASTES	65
IX	READY TO SPRING	73
X	A NARROW ESCAPE	82
XI	IN PERIL OF THEIR LIVES	88
XII	BURIED ALIVE	95
XIII	JUST IN TIME	101
XIV	CLOSE TO DEATH	109
XV	TROUBLE BREWING	114
XVI	THE TRAIL GROWS WARM	121
XVII	A NIGHT OF TERROR	128
XVIII	THE MYSTERIOUS MOUNDS	135
XIX	A WONDERFUL DISCOVERY	142
XX	TAKEN BY SURPRISE	149
XXI	THE CONFESSION	154
XXII	FOLLOWING THE CLUE	159
XXIII	PURSUED	167
XXIV	AGAINST HEAVY ODDS	173
XXV	GREAT NEWS FOR DON	179

CHAPTER I

A COWARDLY ATTACK

"IT certainly is a great idea, to cross the Sahara Desert by car," remarked Captain Frank Sturdy, as he sat on the shaded veranda of an Algerian hotel and looked out on the shimmering sea of sand stretching away to the horizon.

"I believe it has been broached," replied Professor Amos Bruce, setting down the glass of lemonade which he had been sipping. "And whoever conceived it had plenty of nerve, supposing, of course, that he were willing to face the danger himself. It would be a mighty risky project."

"That's just what makes the idea of it so alluring," affirmed the captain, with a smile and an adventurous glint in his eyes. "I wouldn't give a copper for anything that didn't have some risk connected with it. And I don't think it would be such a forlorn hope at that. It seems to me entirely possible."

"Y-e-s, it might be done," assented the professor dubiously. "But it would mean a nerve-racking journey of over two thousand miles."

"Gee, that sounds good to me, Uncle Frank!" broke in Don Sturdy, a tall, muscular boy of fourteen, who had been listening intently to the discussion. "What a lot of wonderful things a fellow would see on a trip like that!"

"No doubt of that," replied his uncle. "But a

good many of the things you'd see wouldn't be pleasant to look upon. Suppose something went wrong with your car and left you stranded a thousand miles from nowhere?"

"Or suppose," added the professor, "you were attacked by some of the many bandits that roam the Sahara? From all accounts, those fellows are mighty bad medicine."

"But people are travelling over the desert all the time, and they get through somehow," said Don, upon whom the idea had taken a hold that was as strong as it was sudden.

"To be sure," agreed the professor. "But they know the desert in all its moods as no outsider can. They are seasoned to the blazing heat of an African Sun. They know the signs of an approaching sand-storm. They are familiar with all the oases and wells on the route. And where their own knowledge and reasoning fall short, the instinct of the camels comes to their help. In every way they have a tremendous advantage over those who were not born sons of the desert."

"There's a good deal in what you say, Amos," said Captain Sturdy. "Yet, after all, I'd back modern science against native experience and habit. It's the outsiders, after all, who do things. Who discovered the North Pole? Not the Eskimos, but an outsider. Who are trying to climb Mt. Everest, the highest peak in the world? Not the natives of the Himalayas, but outsiders. And I'm willing to bet that a car expedition across the Sahara would add more to the world's knowledge than all the contributions by Arabs since the world began."

"It may be, it may be, Frank," admitted the professor. "At any rate, we'll let it go at that. It's too hot a day to argue about anything."

"That's so obviously true that I'm not going to dispute it," laughed the captain, as he settled back in his chair and wiped the perspiration from his forehead.

It was mid-afternoon, and the sun was still beating down fiercely on the little Algerian town of Tuggurt, on the edge of the great Sahara Desert. Most of the inhabitants of the place were taking their afternoon siesta, and the group of three Americans, who had not acquired the habit of sleeping in the daytime, had the hotel veranda to themselves.

The outstanding figure of the three was Captain Frank Sturdy, who lived, when at home, in an old stone house that had been in the family for generations, at Hillville, in an Eastern State, about fifty miles from New York.

He was a big man, but the bigness lay in his great frame and his thews and muscles, for he had not an ounce of superfluous flesh on him. The natural swarthiness of his complexion had been still further darkened by the suns of many climes, for he had travelled over thousands of miles of Africa and Asia as a hunter of big game. His reputation as a fearless hunter and a crack shot was internationally known, and of recent years he had been in great request by zoological gardens and menageries who wished to secure specimens for their collections.

The other man of the party, Professor Amos Regor Bruce, differed widely from his companion in size and appearance. He was of small build, and had mild grey eyes and greyer hair. His profession was that of an archæologist, and he was extremely learned in his speciality. Several degrees had been conferred upon him by American and foreign universities in recognition of his contributions to science.

Don Sturdy, the boy member of the trio, was a strong, well-built boy of the athletic type, with brown hair and eyes, unusually adept in the sports that appeal to a boy of his age. He, too, was a crack shot, this accomplishment being due to his natural aptitude combined with the tutelage of Captain Sturdy, who had spared no pains to make his nephew as good a rifleman as himself.

Don was supposed to be an orphan, due to a tragedy which, as far as anyone knew, had robbed him of his parents some time before. His father, Richard Sturdy, a noted explorer, his mother, Alice, and his sister, Ruth, the latter two years younger than Don, had left the United States on an expedition on the exploring ship *Mercury*. This ship disappeared while on its way around Cape Horn, South America, and had never since been heard of. Repeated inquiries had failed to elicit any news of her, and as time passed on it was generally accepted that she had sunk, with all on board.

The blow was a terrible one to Don, who had loved his parents and sister dearly, and he had never become reconciled to it. Despite all evidence to the contrary, he still hoped against hope that some-where they were still alive, though deep in his heart he knew how slender was the foundation on which that hope rested.

Captain Sturdy, a brother of Don's father, had assumed the guardianship of the boy, and had done his best to take the place of his parents. Professor Bruce, who was Don's uncle on his mother's side, had exercised a careful supervision over his studies.

At the time this story opens, both uncles had accepted propositions from the International Museum and Menagerie Collection Corporation, with offices in London, Paris and New York. Captain Sturdy was to collect rare specimens of animals and Professor Bruce was to secure relics of early African civilisations. Don had pleaded so earnestly to be taken along that at last, though with considerable hesitation, his uncles had consented.

The heat became less intolerable as the afternoon wore on, and the little town began to show some signs of life. The natives emerged from their mud huts, the streets became more frequented, and the flag, that had hung listlessly on the staff over the French Government building, stirred faintly in the merest zephyr of a breeze.

"Possible to live once more," remarked the professor, with a sigh of relief, as he rose from his chair. "Guess I'll hunt up that fellow that told me he knew something about the Cemetery of the Elephants."

"What is that?" asked Don, with interest.

"It may be a reality or it may be a myth," answered his uncle. "If a myth, it's based upon the well-known fact that elephants, when they feel that they are about to die, steal away from the herd and hunt for some secluded spot where they can pass away in peace. The story goes that there's a spot in the Sahara that contains so many elephant bodies that it's a regular cemetery. One of the reasons for my coming here was to ascertain what basis of fact there may be in the story. Had a native tell me yesterday that he knew something about it, but he was called away before he could go into details. Ten to one he really knows nothing about it; then again he may, and I can't afford to overlook anything that may give me a clue."

He went along the veranda to the door of the hotel, and Captain Sturdy looked rather quizzically at Don.

"While your Uncle Amos is looking up the dead, suppose we get after something that's a little livelier," he suggested.

Don was instantly all animation.

"You mean hunting, Uncle Frank?" he asked eagerly.

"Just that," assented his uncle. "I'm getting a bit rusty myself, and I know you're anxious to try that new rifle I bought for you just before we started."

"You bet I am!" exclaimed Don, his eyes sparkling. "What do you suppose we can get around here?"

"Nothing in the way of big game," returned the captain. "We can't go far from town in the hour or so we shall have before nightfall. But we may get a crack at a jackal or two, and then there's a species of fox in this vicinity whose skin I'd like to get. So we'll go in and get our rifles and take a little jaunt."

They suited the action to the word, and in a few minutes were ready to start. They took no guide, for they did not intend to go far from the outskirts of the town.

"I've heard that game can be found sometimes in the vicinity of that sand ridge," said the captain, pointing to an elevation about a mile away. "I'll go towards one side of it and you towards the other, and between us we may get something to pay us for our trouble. But be sure to keep in sight of me and of the town."

Don promised, and they parted, pursuing different routes over the soft sand, though taking care that they should not be at any time more than half a mile apart.

Don walked along, keenly alert for anything on that wide expanse that might promise him a target. Suddenly his heart gave a thump, as he caught sight of a dark object. But his elation left him when a second glance resolved the mass into several human figures.

"Just natives," he murmured in disgust.

He looked again, and his interest quickened. A struggle seemed to be going on. Arms were uplifted as if to strike. Still he was sceptical as to the matter being one of any special importance.

"Such an excitable bunch," he said to himself. "They go up in the air about nothing. Arguing perhaps about something that isn't worth a hill of beans."

He turned to go in the opposite direction, but a

loud cry halted him. He could not distinguish its meaning, save that it seemed to convey an urgent appeal for help.

Don's sight was unusually keen, and as he focused it upon the scene he became aware that two of the group were attacking a third. The latter was doing all he could to defend himself, but he was smaller than either of the others, and it was plain that he was badly overmatched.

Under ordinary circumstances, caution would have prompted David to give a wide berth to a quarrel between natives that was none of his concern. But, as he looked, he discovered something that made him throw prudence to the winds.

The two larger ones—native Algerians, by their dress—were attacking a boy, who was not a native! A white boy like himself! Perhaps an American boy!

Don fired one shot in the air to attract the attention of his uncle. The next instant, he was rushing towards the struggling group, waving his rifle and yelling like an Indian.

CHAPTER II

TO THE RESCUE

At the sound of the shot the natives turned quickly, and for a moment suspended their attack, though they still kept one on either side of the boy to prevent his escape. Don was a fast runner, and although the shifting sands offered an unstable footing, he was soon in close proximity to the men, both of whom had drawn their knives and thrown themselves into an attitude of defence. The boy whom they were assailing had made a movement as though to run towards Don, but one of the men caught him and threw him roughly to the ground. When within twenty feet, Don checked his speed and brought his rifle to bear.

"Clear out and leave that boy alone!" he shouted.

Although the natives could not understand the words, the tone and the gesture left no doubt as to their meaning. Had Don been unarmed, they would undoubtedly have stood their ground, depending upon their superior size and strength. But the weapon compelled respect, and they were fully aware that against it their knives offered but little promise of a successful outcome of a struggle.

For a moment they stood uncertainly, taking counsel with each other in a growling undertone. Then, concluding that discretion was the better part of valour and hastened towards that conclusion by a forward step and a repeated command of Don, they drew off, showing their teeth in a snarl like that of a wolf.

Don lowered his rifle and turned towards the boy he had come to help. But just then terror leaped into the latter's eyes, and he shouted in a voice that rose almost to a shriek.

"Look out! Look out! Drop!"

Like a flash, Don went down. And not a second too soon, for a sharp rock came whizzing over his head and buried itself some distance off in the sand. He leaped to his feet to see the two men running away at the top of their speed. He threw his rifle to his shoulder and ran his eye over the barrel to the sight.

At that distance he could have brought either one of them down. But even with his finger on the trigger, he paused. Had they been running towards him he would have fired. But the danger was over, and no matter how much they deserved it, he could not shoot them down like rabbits.

As the men sped away in the direction of the town, Don rushed forward and helped the boy to his feet. The latter was panting from his tussle with his assailants and with excitement, and though he tried to speak, his words were slow in coming.

His face was bruised from blows and his clothes were torn from the rough handling that he had undergone. His hair, which was of a fiery red, was shaggy and unkempt and partly covered his face. But his eyes were blue, and Don's heart gave a leap as he recognised that the boy was white and that his features looked like those of an American.

"They were giving you rather a rough deal," Don said kindly, as he steadied the lad on his feet.

"They sure were," the boy returned in English. "And I'm mighty thankful that you came along just as you did. I was just about all in." The accent, as well as the slang, was undeniably American.

"So you come from the same country that I do," cried Don, in delight.

"Sure thing," was the reply, accompanied by a grin.

"That makes me doubly glad that I happened along just when I did," said Don. "What's your name and where do you come from?"

"My name is Teddy Allison, and I used to live in New York."

"New York!" exclaimed Don. "Better and better. Why, I live only fifty miles from New York. My name is Don Sturdy. Shake."

The two lads shook hands heartily, and were friends from that moment.

"What were those fellows trying to do to you?" asked Don, as they seated themselves on the sand to await the coming of Captain Sturdy, who, alarmed by the shot, was hurrying in their direction, though still some distance away.

"Trying to rob me," replied Teddy, brushing some of the sand from his fiery mop of hair. "Don't look much as though I were worth robbing, do I?" he demanded, with a wide grin. "But I have one thing worth stealing," he went on, drawing a heavy gold watch from his pocket. "It used to belong to my father"—here a shadow crossed his face that Don was quick to notice—"and in this country, where they'd steal the pennies off a dead man's eyes, I suppose it would seem like a fortune. These fellows had probably seen me draw it out when I was in the town, and they've watched me and followed me this afternoon when I came out here for a stroll. I had noticed them loitering about, but didn't think anything about it until they closed in on me."

"I noticed you were putting up a mighty stiff fight," remarked Don admiringly.

"I wasn't going to let go of it without a struggle," replied Teddy modestly. "And that not only because of its value, but because it used to belong to my father. Of course, the odds were against me and it was only a matter of time before they would have got it if you hadn't happened along. I suppose they would have knifed me, if they couldn't have got it in any other way. Life is pretty cheap in this country. I can't thank you enough for scaring them off. They didn't like the looks of that gun."

"I'm glad it wasn't necessary to use it," returned Don simply.

"You're likely to have to use it if you stay in this country very long," predicted Teddy. "What brought you all the way from America to this jumping-off place, anyway?"

"I came here with my uncles," replied Don. "There's one of them now, coming towards us. The other's at the hotel. They're on an exploring and collecting expedition. But now let me ask you the same question. What brought you here?"

Again the shadow that Don had noted came on Teddy's face, and this time it stayed.

"I came with my father," he said. "My mother died so long ago that I don't remember her, and father was so restless after that that he was travelling almost all the time. I suppose there's hardly a place in the world that he hasn't been in at some time or other. On this last trip he brought me along."

"Oh, well, as long as your father is with you, you're all right," said Don, while a pain like a stab went through his heart at the thought that he himself had no father with him.

"But he isn't with me," explained Teddy, with a little catch in his voice.

"How's that?" asked Don, in surprise. "You don't mean to say that he'd leave you in a place like this all alone?"

"He wouldn't if he could help it," said Teddy. "He——"

"Hallo, Don!" came a shout from Captain Sturdy, now within calling distance. "Are you all right?"

"All right, Uncle Frank," Don shouted back, and, excusing himself to Teddy for a moment, he rose and ran to meet the captain.

"Sure nothing happened to you?" his uncle asked as he came up. "It gave me a start when I heard that shot and saw you running and yelling."

"I'm not a bit hurt," Don reassured him. "Just had a bit of an adventure, and made a friend in the course of it."

The captain looked a little bewildered.

"Is that the friend you're talking about?" he asked, as his glance fell on Teddy.

"No one else," replied Don. "What do you think,

Uncle Frank, of meeting a New York boy in the Desert of Sahara?"

By this time they had come up to Teddy.

"This is Captain Sturdy, one of my uncles I was telling you about, Teddy," Don said, by way of introduction. "Uncle Frank, this is Teddy Allison."

Teddy shyly reached out his hand and the captain took it heartily.

"Any friend of Don's is a friend of mine," he said, with a smile. "You've certainly met under unusual circumstances. And you seem to have been pretty badly bruised. What's happened to you?"

"A couple of natives tried to rob me," explained Teddy. "And I guess they'd have done it all right if Don here hadn't come along with his gun and made them fly. There they are now," and he pointed to the two figures, rapidly vanishing in the direction of the town.

The captain looked at Don with pride.

"So you drove them off all by your lonesome?" he said. "Good for you, my boy. Did they show fight?"

"They pulled out their knives all right," put in Teddy, "and one of them threw a sharp rock at Don, just missing him. Then they ran off."

With a few brief questions, the captain brought out all the details of the affair.

"Those rascals ought to be arrested," he said. "I'll report the matter to the French head of the police. Though since the natives look so much alike to our eyes, I suppose you'd have difficulty in identifying them even if they were caught. But come along now and I'll take you back to your folks. I suppose they're staying at the hotel."

"I—I haven't any folks," stammered Teddy. "That is, white folks. I'm staying in one of the huts with a native, an Arab, Alam Bokaru, his name is."

For a moment the captain was stunned.

"No folks!" he ejaculated. "Thousands of miles from home and only an Arab to take care of you! My poor boy! Tell me all about it."

The kindness in Captain Sturdy's tone brought tears to Teddy's eyes and he turned away to hide them.

"Teddy was telling me just when you came up," Don broke in, to give the boy time to get control of himself, "that he was brought to this country by his father."

"And your father is dead?" asked the captain gently.

"I don't know," replied Teddy, who had by this time mastered his emotion. "He was captured by the natives, and the last I saw of him he was being taken towards some mountains. They may have killed him, or they may have made a slave of him. I don't know."

"Were you with him at the time?" queried the captain, profoundly touched and interested.

"Yes," replied Teddy. "My father started from here with a small caravan to go to the Hoggar Mountains, taking me along with him. Everything was all right for the first two weeks. We had water and provisions enough, and although it was awfully hot, we got along by sleeping in the daytime and doing most of our travelling by night.

"But one night, just as we were starting on, a party of Arabs came down on us. There were a good many more of them than we had in our party. Then, too, they took us by surprise. There was a good deal of yelling and shooting, and some were killed. In the end, they got the best of us, and our people scattered. One of the men, the master of the camels, who was fond of my father, grabbed me and carried me away to a hiding place among some rocks, though I was kicking and struggling all the time, trying to get to my father. But the man said I would be killed, and he wouldn't let me go. From where we were, we saw the fellows who had been fighting us going away with the camels and our baggage and provisions. My father was tied on one of the camels. He—he——" and here Teddy's voice choked and he could go no further.

"Poor boy!" said the captain, as he threw his arm around the lad's shoulders. "You've had a hard time of it. But now pluck up your courage. At least, your father's alive, and while there's life there's hope."

"Do you think he's still alive?" cried Teddy eagerly.

"I feel sure of it," declared the captain. "If they'd wanted to kill him, they'd have done it on the spot without taking the trouble to carry him off. The Arabs are quick workers in any case like that. Maybe they hope to get ransom for him. Tell me this, my boy, and don't think I'm trying to pry into your affairs. Did your father have money, property—enough to buy his liberty, if that should prove to be their game?"

"I—I don't know," said Teddy, with a boy's vagueness as to money affairs. "He always seemed to have plenty. In New York we had a big house and a butler and other servants. But I've heard him say that he'd never have to hustle for money again if he could only find the Cave of Emeralds."

CHAPTER III

THE MASTER OF CAMELS

CAPTAIN STURDY gave a start and a sudden exclamation.

"What's that you said," he asked, eyeing Teddy keenly. "Find what?"

"The Cave of Emeralds," repeated Teddy, in some surprise at the captain's quickened interest. "You know, the cave that's in the Hoggar Mountains and has a lot of treasure hidden in it. That's what father was looking for when he was captured."

"What made him think he could find it?" asked the captain, the spirit of adventure that Don knew so well coming into his eyes.

"He had a map," answered Teddy. "He got it in some way from an old Bedouin chief. I don't know much about it, but I've often seen him bending over it and studying it for hours at a time. I know he felt sure he was going to find the cave on this trip."

For a few moments the captain stood silent,

evidently thinking deeply. Then he roused himself, for he noticed how quickly the darkness was coming on.

"We've got to get back to town," he said, picking up his rifle and leading the way. "Come, Don. Come along, Teddy. By the way, can't you come with us to the hotel? I'm going to take charge of you now, if you are willing, until we can find your father."

"Oh, are you going to look for him?" cried Teddy, delight coming into his eyes.

"Are you really, Uncle Frank?" exclaimed Don, with an excitement almost equal to that of Teddy himself.

"Of course I am," replied the captain emphatically. "Do you suppose that I, an American, can let another American remain in the power of a lot of rascally bandits if it's in any way possible to rescue him? I'll try to get the French authorities here to do something. I'll make efforts to get our own country interested in his behalf. And, by ginger, if it's necessary, I'll go and hunt for him myself!" he ended explosively.

"Oh, if you do, I'll never forget it as long as I live!" declared Teddy.

Don had been profoundly moved by Teddy's story. He would have felt deep sympathy for him in any event, but he was especially affected because it brought to his mind his own great loss. It was even greater than that of his newly found friend. Teddy had not been conscious of his mother's death, and his present grief concerned only his father. But Don, at one blow, had lost, as far as he knew to the contrary, father, mother and sister. And the tragedy of that probable loss had come to him with redoubled force, as he listened to Teddy's narrative. His heart was torn with pain and grief.

He was aroused from the bitter contemplation of his loss by the captain's voice.

"You haven't answered my question, Teddy. Are you coming along with us to the hotel now? Or will you come over later?"

"I think," said Teddy, with a little hesitation, "that I'd better not come just now, though I'd love to. But Alam and his wife will be worried about me if I don't get back there pretty soon. They've been awfully good to me, and I don't want to do anything that will make them feel bad."

"Right you are, my boy," agreed the captain heartily. "I think all the more of you for thinking of your old friends and not forgetting them for the new. Where does this Alam live?"

"In the native quarter, about half a mile from the hotel," answered Teddy.

"Well," said the captain, "suppose you go home to supper. A little later come over to the hotel and bring Alam with you. I'm curious to see the man who has been so kind to you. Then, too, I want to thank him in the name of all Americans for what he has done for an American boy."

"I'll tell him," promised Teddy. "I think very likely he'll come. But I'll be there anyway."

By this time they had reached the outskirts of the town, and here they parted, Teddy going through one of the narrow streets that turned off towards the native quarter, while Don and his uncle pursued their way to the hotel. They found Professor Bruce waiting for them, not a little uneasy because of their prolonged absence.

"What on earth kept you so long?" he asked. "A little while longer, and I'd have organised a party to look for you."

"Sorry to have worried you, Amos," returned the captain. "A rather unusual thing occurred and delayed us. But let's go in to dinner now, and while we're eating we'll tell you all about it."

Don was so excited that he paid very little attention to the meal. He was even content to let Captain Sturdy tell the story and he listened to his uncles discussing the event in which he had played so large a part. The professor showed keen interest in the captain's narrative, and when he had heard the whole story sat silent for some time toying absently with his spoon while his coffee remained untasted.

"Well, what do you think of it, Amos?" asked Captain Sturdy.

The professor roused himself from his abstraction.

"I think you did right in promising the poor lad to help rescue his father," he said. "I'm with you heart and soul in that, although it lets us in for a pretty big contract. And of course we'll take the boy under our guardianship until we find his father or restore him to his friends or relatives in America. Poor little chap! He's had a hard row to hoe."

"What do you think about this Cave of Emeralds?" asked the captain.

"It's a mighty romantic story," was the reply. "It sounds to me something like the pot of gold at the end of the rainbow. Still, there may be something in it. From the boy's story, it seems that his father had something practical to go upon, or he would never have undertaken such a hazardous expedition; and I've seen so many wonderful things in these Eastern lands that I seldom say that anything's impossible on first hearing."

"The whole thing will stand a lot of hard thinking," returned the captain. "But I think we can make it fit in fairly well with the purpose for which we came to the Sahara. Our plans, you know, comprised a trip to the Hoggar Plateau, in the heart of the desert, and it's somewhere in that vicinity that Teddy's father was captured. We'll be able to hunt for him without turning much aside from our original plans. It's somewhere in that Hoggar district, probably, that the Cave of Emeralds lies, if it exists at all. It was towards that the party was heading when the raid occurred.

"I don't know when anything has taken a stronger hold on me than that matter of the emeralds," went on the captain. "Precious stones have always had a fascination for me just for their beauty, the liquid light that sparkles in them."

"To say nothing of the glittering gold coin for which they may be exchanged," remarked the professor, with a smile.

"Oh, that's not to be scorned either," admitted the captain, laughing. "Think of it, Amos! It would make us rich for life. You could devote yourself to science just for its own sake. I could roam anywhere I chose all over the surface of the globe. And Don here——"

"I could travel everywhere looking for my father and mother and sister!" broke in Don a little unsteadily, expressing the wish that was ever uppermost in his heart.

There was silence for a moment as their thoughts went out after the missing ones, inexpressibly dear to them all.

"Well," said the professor, rousing himself, "it seems worth an effort. It's a well-known fact that in ancient times emeralds were comparatively abundant in this region, and some are still found here. The story may have a foundation in fact. But it will be no light task. The Sahara itself is almost as large as all Europe, and the Hoggar Plateau is a terrible district, full of chasms, precipices, and peopled by robbers."

"Yet the Cave of Emeralds is probably in that very region," remarked the captain.

"It's in that direction, too, that the Cemetery of Elephants is to be found, if what I heard this afternoon is true," returned the professor. "You remember that when I left you, I told you I was going to hunt up a native who seemed to know something about it?"

"Yes, I remember," replied the captain. "But you didn't seem very sanguine about getting any genuine information."

"Well, I found him, and I was agreeably disappointed," was the reply. "He's really one of the most intelligent natives I've had the luck to come across. Steeped in superstition, of course, like all of them, but outside of that he was very keen and well informed. Seems to know the desert like a book.

Sort of camel breaker by profession; master of camels, is the title he goes by."

"Do you remember his name?" asked Don eagerly.

"He told me what it was, but I don't know that I can recall it," replied the professor. "Some outlandish name—Salaam or something like that."

"Was it Alam Bokaru?" asked Don, his eyes shining with excitement.

"That sounds like it," replied the professor, a little surprised. "Why?"

"Because that's probably the man who saved Teddy from the bandits," answered Don. "That was the name Teddy mentioned, and he said that he was a master of camels."

"Is that so?" exclaimed the professor with interest. "Well, if he's the man, Teddy couldn't have fallen into better hands. He struck me as an upright, self-respecting man—much superior to the usual run of natives with whom I have come in contact."

"I hope he comes with Teddy to-night," said Don.

"So do I," returned the professor. "I want not only to thank him for what he has done for an American boy, but also to get some more information from him. This is not the land of hustle and push, and it takes time to learn anything from the natives."

"Perhaps Alam knows something about the Cave of Emeralds," put in Don.

"Quite possible," assented the captain, rising from the table, while the others followed his example. "We'd better go up to our sitting-room now and wait for him—that is, if Teddy brings him along with him."

"Couldn't we wait for him on the veranda, or, better yet, on the roof?" suggested Don. "It would be ever so much cooler."

"I know it would," returned the captain, with a smile. "But when we get to talking about hidden treasure, it'll be safer to be within four walls."

They went up to their suite, the captain having left word with the clerk that he expected visitors and that they were to be sent directly up to him when they came. It was not long before a tap came on the door, and Don sprang to open it.

"Come right in, Teddy," he said, when he saw his new comrade standing there a little abashed. "Bring your friend with you," he added, as he saw a tall figure in native garb standing beside him.

The two visitors entered the room, and the captain and professor rose to greet them.

"So you've come, Teddy," said the captain, taking him by the hand. "This is Don's other uncle, Professor Bruce, whom we've told all about you."

The professor greeted Teddy with a friendliness and sympathy that put the latter immediately at ease.

"And this," continued the captain, with a friendly nod towards the Arab, into whose eyes had come a look of pleased recognition as they fell on the professor, "is, I suppose, the man to whom you owe your life."

"Yes," said Teddy gratefully, "the man who has been like a second father to me—Alam Bokaru, master of camels."

They exchanged salutations, the Arab bowing in

a stately manner, which, while it expressed a touch of deference, had in it no taint of servility.

He was a tall, spare man with a pair of flashing, black eyes, an aquiline nose and a regularity of feature that betrayed Arab blood without any admixture. There was about him a certain dignity that commanded respect. Courage and self-reliance were plainly manifest in face and manner. He conveyed the impression of one who could be a steadfast friend and a dangerous enemy.

He refused a chair, but seated himself upon some pillows that the captain pulled off the lounge. His English was imperfect, and though he could understand much that was said to him in that language, he spoke it with hesitation. This was no bar to conversation, however, for the professor spoke Arabic almost like a native, and the captain knew enough of it for ordinary purposes. So that it was in that language that most of the talk was conducted.

After the Americans had thanked him warmly in the name of their countrymen for what he had done for Teddy, the professor launched into the matters that he and the captain had talked over at table.

During the animated conversation that followed, the captain listened intently, catching its import only in part, while Don and Teddy chatted together in a corner of the room.

"Don," asked Teddy, "did your uncle, Captain Sturdy, mean that I should come here to the hotel to stay with you?"

"He certainly did, Teddy."

"Gee, how nice that would be after staying in Alam's house! But, Don, they've been awfully good to me, and I saw at supper time that Alam's wife would think it impolite if I left so suddenly—she'd call me a barbarian," and the boy chuckled. "I guess I'd better go back to-night and take a longer time to say ' thank you ' and ' good-bye.'"

"All right. You know best about that. I'll tell Uncle Frank and Uncle Amos."

At last a pause came in the talk between Professor Bruce and Alam, and the captain broke in with a question.

"How about it, Amos?" he asked.

"Well," said the professor, with a wry smile, "he says that we may find the Cemetery of Elephants. He says we may find Teddy's father. He says we may find the Cave of Emeralds. But there's one thing he's sure we'll find."

"What's that?" asked the captain eagerly.

"Death!"

CHAPTER IV

THE CITY OF BRASS

At that ominous word death Captain Sturdy started from his chair, and Don and Teddy stopped short in their conversation.

"Death!" exclaimed the captain incredulously. "What does he mean by that? It isn't necessarily fatal to make a trip into the Sahara. Danger, yes. But death? Nonsense!"

"It isn't the physical dangers of the trip he has in mind," explained the professor. "It's just a superstitious idea of his. He says that the City of Brass lies somewhere in that region, and that it would mean death to any mortal who looked on it."

"The City of Brass!" exclaimed Don. "I never heard of that. What is it and where is it?"

"It's supposed to be a very great and wonderful city of ancient times that existed in the heart of the Sahara," replied the professor. "Tradition says that it was built by people who once ruled over all Northern Africa—the 'Sons of Ad,' the Arabs called them.

"At that time, the Sahara was very different from what it is now. There were great lakes of fresh water, dense woods and fertile valleys. But, according to the story, the people became so wise and powerful and haughty that after that they defied

Allah. So Allah put their land under a blight and wiped out the race. But their great city still stands somewhere in the desert."

"Allah is great," murmured Alam Bokaru.

The captain sniffed unbelievingly.

"Just a fairy tale," he remarked. "One of the legends without any basis that all people have. I don't believe a word of it."

"I wouldn't dismiss it quite so contemptuously as that, Frank," said the professor mildly. "Of course, we can put aside the idea of death being visited on any one who might catch a glimpse of the city. That's pure superstition. But it may be barely possible that such a place exists. Enough has already been found to indicate that the Sahara was once the centre of a great civilisation. Most of the relics of it have been blotted out by the drifting sands. But the City of Brass may have been so located—in a mountainous section perhaps—that it has escaped this general obliteration."

"What slightest proof have we got of it?" snorted the captain.

"There's a pretty circumstantial account that in the year A.D. 700, in the reign of the Caliph Abd-al-Malik, an expedition was sent out that found it and brought home a great deal of treasure from it," said the professor slowly.

"Just an Arabian Nights story!" the captain exclaimed.

"Perhaps," agreed the professor. "Although the story is told with such remarkable detail that it sounds as though it might have been written by a conscientious modern reporter who had a reputation for veracity to maintain and put things down just as he saw them.

"Then, too, there's Sir Richard Burton, the English explorer, who lived among the Arabs so long that he became almost like one of them, and even made the journey to Mecca, which would have meant death to him if he had been discovered.

"He says that he talked personally to two men who claimed to have seen the City of Brass. He afterwards investigated the stories of three others who claimed to have seen it in a mirage. All the accounts tallied, although the narrators were unknown to each other—the same description of a city with glittering brass or copper towers and buildings shining in the sun. Burton believed the stories were substantially true. And Burton was a pretty shrewd man."

"He just believed them because he wanted to," declared the captain. "The wish was father to the thought."

"Allah is great," put in Alam Bokaru. "The thing is true."

The Americans looked at him curiously for a moment, and then the professor resumed:

"Not much more than thirty years ago, just before the Great War, the Egyptian Government was fitting out an expedition under the leadership of an English explorer to discover, if possible, the City of Brass. The plan was based on information brought by two Arabs who claimed to have entered the city and brought back with them treasures to prove it. These two men agreed to lead the exploring expedition to the place."

"But you notice they didn't do it," said the captain, with a touch of sarcasm.

"That was no fault of theirs," was the reply. "The Senussi people heard of the project and made such dire threats that the Egyptian Government called the matter off."

"It stands to reason," declared the captain, still unconvinced, "that if there really were such a city, someone who could be relied on would have found it before this. Many explorers have crossed the Sahara."

"Oh, I don't know," replied the professor. "The Sahara isn't altogether the flat waste of sand that most people think. There are chasms and cliffs and gorges and sunken oases in which hundreds of such cities might be concealed, and, except by the merest luck, an explorer might never run across them."

"Allah is great," repeated Alam. "The City of Brass is in the desert. But Allah guards the secret and death will come to him who looks upon it."

The professor turned to the impassive Arab.

"How did your people first happen to run across the City of Brass and what did they find there, Alam?" he asked.

Probably flattered by the request, although his features remained immobile, Alam bowed, and began a queer sort of singsong chant. At intervals he would stop, and then the professor would translate what he had said.

The captain listened with a sceptical smile, but Don and Teddy hung breathlessly on every word.

"They drew near the city," said Alam, after having described the fitting out of the expedition, "and behold, it was, as it were, a piece of a mountain or a mass of brass cast in a mould. And impenetrable, for the height of its walls and bulwarks. It shone out like fire under the sun. So they ascended the highest hill which overlooked the city. When they reached the top they beheld beneath them a city. Never saw eyes a greater or goodlier, with dwelling places and mansions of towering height, with palaces and pavilions and domes gleaming gloriously bright.

"When they scaled the walls, they found the place filled with the dead. They beheld the merchants sitting on the shop boards, dead, with shrivelled skin. Silks and brocades, laden with red gold and white silver, the owners lying dead upon mats of scented goat leather and looking as if they would speak. They traversed a street of pearls and rubies, of emeralds and topaz and other jewels, and shops full of gold and silver. They came upon a palace and in the vestibule stood benches of ivory plated with glittering gold, whereon lay men whose skin had dried up on their bones. For lack of food they had perished.

"You see," said the professor, after the pause necessary to put this in English, "the dead had been mummified, apparently by the hot dry air of the Sahara. The place had probably been in a fertile section, but some violent change in climate had destroyed vegetation, and the population had perished of famine."

"What a fearful death!" murmured Don.

"I should say so," added Teddy, with a shiver.

"They passed through a corridor," continued

Alam, on a nod from the professor, "paved with marble and hung with veil-like tapestries, embroidered with all manner of beasts and birds whose bodies were of red gold and white silver, and their eyes of pearls and rubies.

"Many marvels they saw, and came at last to a domed pavilion, on which lay the body of a woman. She wore a tight-fitting body robe of fine pearls, with a crown of red gold on her head. There was a golden tablet on one of the steps leading to the couch on which the body of the woman lay, and on this tablet was written——"

Here Alam stopped, while the professor translated.

"Oh, he stopped at just the wrong place!" cried Don impulsively. "I'm crazy to hear what was on the tablet."

"That's a sign that Alam is a good story-teller," observed the captain, who was himself by this time almost as breathlessly interested as the boys themselves. "He wants to keep you in suspense. A sort of 'continued in our next,' as it were."

That Alam had not been wholly without guile in this was indicated by his deliberation before he resumed:

"Thus read the tablet:

"I am Tadmurah, daughter of the kings of the Amalekites. I possessed that which never king possessed. Thus lived I many years in all ease and delight of life till Death knocked at my door and to me and my folk fell calamities. There betided us seven successive years of drought wherein no drop of rain fell on us from the skies and no green thing sprouted for us on the face of the earth. So we ate what was with us of victual, then we fell upon the cattle and devoured them until nothing was left. Thereupon I let bring my treasures and sent out trusted men to buy food.

"They circuited all the lands in quest thereof and left no city unsought, but found it not to be bought. They returned to us with the treasure after a long absence. They gave us to know that they could not succeed in bartering fine pearls for poor wheat, bushel for bushel, weight for weight.

"One party, however, came not back—the men to whom had been entrusted the emeralds. Whither they went or why they returned not no one knoweth. Perhaps a storm overtook them and the gods claimed them."

The captain sat bolt upright as this was translated. "Emeralds!" he ejaculated. The professor put his finger on his lips, and Alam went on:

"So when we despaired of succour, we displayed all our riches and things of price, and, shutting the gates of the city and its strong places, resigned ourselves. Then we all died as thou seest us, and left what we had builded and what we had hoarded."

The speaker ceased, and indicated with a gesture that that was all.

"Well, Frank," said the professor, with a smile, after he had translated the concluding words, "there's the story. What do you think of it?"

Don expected to hear a scornful repudiation of the tale from the captain's lips, but he was mistaken. It was evident that his uncle had been shaken from his stubborn attitude by the precise details of the story.

"There's a certain ring of truth about it," he conceded slowly. "Either the man who first told it was a painstaking reporter of what he had actually seen or he was a most magnificent and convincing liar. In any case, we have to hand it to him for being an artist in his line."

"We have to admit that there's nothing impossible about it, however wild and improbable it seems," mused the professor. "We know that great cities have sometimes been wiped out by famine. Why might not the City of Brass have been one of them?"

"Allah is great," murmured Alam. "The story is true."

"Why did Alam tell you that death would be the portion of anyone who should discover it?" asked the captain. "The fellows who first saw it got back safely, according to the story. Why shouldn't anyone else?"

"That's a later tradition," explained the professor. "Alam told me that his father and grandfather told him so. And in this country that's proof enough for anything."

"Allah is great," intoned Alam. "To see it means death."

For a moment the captain kept silent. Then he pounded his fist upon the table.

"I'm going to take a chance," he cried. "That is, of course, Amos, if you are willing."

"What do you mean?" asked the professor.

"I'm going to hunt for the City of Brass! I'm going to look for the Cave of Emeralds!"

CHAPTER V

A DANGEROUS UNDERTAKING

THERE was a stir of excitement in the group at this bold announcement. The professor was jarred out of his usual calm. Don's eyes sparkled and Teddy felt a thrill go through his veins. Only Alam retained his impassivity.

"Hadn't you better think that over twice, Frank?" asked the professor mildly.

"I'm used to making quick decisions," returned the captain. "If I weren't I wouldn't be alive to-day. As it is, I've been thinking it over all the time that Alam has been talking. It will fit right into our plans, anyway. Where we're taking so many risks, one more won't make much difference. From all accounts, this City of Brass, if it exists at all, is in a mountainous region, probably this Hoggar Plateau that we're going to. And you heard what Alam said about the Emeralds in his story of the city. The two things are bound up together. Let's include them in our general scheme. If we find them, all right. If we don't, we won't be any the worse off. What do you say, Amos? Of course, I don't want to rush you off your feet. Sleep on it and let me know what you think in the morning."

That the plan had its appeal to the professor was evident by the glow that came into his cheeks and the speculative look into his eyes.

"I don't know that there would be any objection to making that one of the goals of our trip," said the professor at last. "As you say, failure would not detract from the value of the other objects of our expedition, and if by any chance we should run across this mysterious city, the gain to the world's knowledge would be enormous."

"I should say so!" broke in the captain. "It would cast in the shade all the other discoveries you have ever made, important as they are. It would give you a permanent place in history. Then let's consider it settled that we'll make the attempt to find it."

"Of course, there are Alam's objections to be considered," remarked the professor. "I had rather set my heart on having him come with us as guide. From what I've heard, he knows the desert like a book, and is one of the most trustworthy and dependable of the Arabs in this section. I think very likely we'd be able to obtain his services for all the other objects of the expedition, but he may refuse if he finds we're including the City of Brass among them. You've heard what he's had to say about that."

"Suppose we let that rest for a moment," suggested the captain. "Find out what he knows about the Cave of Emeralds. Has he any definite idea where it is located?"

The professor turned to Alam and conversed with him earnestly for a few minutes.

"He's sure it's somewhere in the Hoggar range," the professor explained. "He knows that Teddy's father believed himself to be within a day's journey from it at the time the raid was made on the caravan. That's about as far as his real knowledge goes."

"That isn't so bad," rejoined the captain. "If he can lead us to the spot where the fight occurred, so that we'll be within a day's march of the cave, we'll have a chance to scout around and find it."

"Or better yet," suggested the professor, "if we can find Teddy's father and he still has the map with him, our task will be made that much easier."

"Right you are," acquiesced the captain. "I think perhaps we'd better not discuss the matter much further to-night. We've already got a good deal of information that we want to think over and digest before we go any further. But there is just one thing that I'm curious about."

"Let's have it," replied the professor.

"It's just this," was the reply. "If Alam is afraid to go with us into that region for fear he may happen to see the City of Brass and so suffer death, how came it that he was ready to go with Mr. Allison into the same district?"

"That's a fair question," returned Professor Bruce. "I'll ask him."

He turned to the Arab and put the question. The reply took several minutes.

"Alam says," stated the professor, "that he went as far as he did because he knew that up to that spot, with which he was perfectly familiar, there was no danger of coming upon the mysterious city. But he would not have gone much farther into the Hoggar range. He would either have made camp to await Mr. Allison's return and let the other go on alone, or, at the very most, he would have followed him only on foot."

"Why on foot?" asked the captain, with a puzzled expression. "Wouldn't that be just as dangerous for him as though he had been on a camel?"

"Not by any means," replied the professor, with the merest suspicion of a smile, which, out of courtesy to his guest, he suppressed instantly. "The threat of death for anyone who sees the City of Brass only applies to mounted men. All others are immune. What are the exact words, Alam?" he asked.

"He who from his camel's back looks upon the City of Brass shall be smitten with death," chanted the Arab. "He and his beast shall fall to the ground together and the vultures shall devour them."

"You see," said the professor. "These people can't conceive of anyone being in the desert except on a camel's back. They take that for granted."

"I see," mused the captain, and into his face came an expression of relief. "I think that solves our problem. I guess there won't be any difficulty in getting Alam to come along as our guide. Can you come and see us again to-morrow night, Alam?" he asked.

"I will come," replied Alam sententiously, as he rose and prepared to depart.

"And you be sure to come around the first thing in the morning, won't you, Teddy?" urged Don, as his new-found friend prepared to accompany Alam.

"You bet I will," replied Teddy enthusiastically.

"Perhaps," he added with a grin, "you'll see more of me than you want to."

"No danger of that," put in the captain genially. "From now on, we regard you as one of the family, and you're going to be under our care until we restore you to your father or to some other of your people."

"I can't thank you enough for all your kindness," said Teddy, his voice trembling a little, as he and Alam left the room and went out into the night.

"I admit, Frank," remarked the professor, when they were left alone, "that you piqued my curiosity a little when you expressed such confidence that we could get Alam to go with us despite his superstitious fears. Just what was your idea?"

"Because if he sees the City of Brass at all, I don't imagine it will be from a camel's back," replied the captain.

"From what, then?" asked the professor, in some surprise, while Don also looked puzzled.

"From the seat of a car," replied the captain.

CHAPTER VI

A GLIMPSE OF OLD ENEMIES

THERE was an exclamation of delight from Don and the professor half started from his chair when they grasped Captain Sturdy's meaning.

"Surely, Frank, you're not in earnest!" Professor Bruce ejaculated.

"Never more so in my life," replied the captain as he glanced with a smile from one to the other.

"Oh, it will be just great, Uncle Frank!" cried Don, almost dancing in his excitement.

"How can a car get through a pathless desert of sand?" objected Professor Bruce. "You couldn't get power enough to drive it along."

"That's true of the ordinary machine," conceded the captain. "But I saw something in the town to-day that has set me thinking. I'm going to make a thorough study of it to-morrow, and then we'll talk it over. Let's defer the matter till then. You and Don come with us. Then we'll know better what we are talking about, and can go into the matter thoroughly."

This was agreed on, though Don was consumed with curiosity and would gladly have stayed up half the night to learn more of what his adventurous uncle had in mind.

Even when the morning dawned, however, he had to restrain his impatience for a while, as the captain's first task was to set whatever agencies he could in motion to bring about the release of Mr Allison from captivity, if he should still be alive.

Captain Sturdy went first to the representative of the French Government and laid the matter before him. That official was polite and sympathetic but not encouraging. The Hoggar Plateau was a long way off, and the difficulties of the task seemed to him almost insuperable. He had only a slender garrison to support his authority, and at the moment could not spare a sufficient number of men to make the search. He promised, however, to communicate with his Government, and perhaps some way could be found to send out an expedition.

From the French Residency, the captain went to the telegraph office and sent a long dispatch to the American representative at Algiers, laying before him all he knew of the mishap of his countryman and urging energetic action in his behalf. He asked that a reply should be sent to him at the earliest possible moment.

For the moment, this was all that could be done, and the captain returned to the hotel for his companions.

"Not much hope from any of these sources, I'm afraid," he remarked to Professor Bruce and Don, as he wiped the perspiration from his brow and dropped into a chair on the veranda. "They would like to help if they could, but their resources in this out-of-the-way place are inadequate. Moreover, their hands are so tied with red tape that months probably would pass before they got started, if they started at all. I guess whatever's done we'll have to do ourselves. But now come along, before it gets too hot."

Just as they were getting ready to go, Teddy came along and received a cordial greeting from all of them.

"Can Teddy come with us?" asked Don eagerly.

"Sure thing," replied the captain, with a genial smile that warmed Teddy's heart. "He's one of the family now, you know, until we find his father."

There was plenty of interest in the little town on the fringe of the desert to keep the boys in a state of keen interest and animation. Even to Teddy, to whom it was familiar, there was something new all the time to see and learn.

Except in the French quarter, there were no paved streets. The roads were winding and narrow, so narrow in places that it was impossible for a vehicle to get through.

"It would be easy for Teddy or me to leap from a housetop of one side of the street to one on the opposite side," observed Don, standing in the street and looking up.

"Don't try it, though," laughed his Uncle Amos.

The houses were mostly made of mud, baked to the consistency of stone under the scorching heat of the African sun. The interiors, they could see as they passed, were dark and small.

"Many of these have no windows, and all the light they get comes through the door!" exclaimed Don.

"The lack of windows is not due to poverty or indifference, but because the light that would stream in would make the rooms intolerably hot," explained Teddy.

Groups of Arab children played about the doors, apparently oblivious of the heat. Men, in garments that had once been white, went to and fro in the street on their daily avocations. Others idled their time away in the coffee houses with which the town was liberally provided. Women, their faces veiled, passed along coming from or going to market. Now and then a camel, groaning and grumbling under his load, went by, his driver walking alongside. There was no hurry or bustle, as in an American or European city.

"If time were money, these fellows would all be millionaires," Don remarked, with a laugh, to Teddy.

There were few shops in the ordinary sense of the word, except some kept by foreign residents. Little strings of shacks without doors extended along the business streets, with the goods displayed where all could see and handle them. Behind the piles of merchandise, the owners sat on cushions and smoked placidly as though they cared little whether they sold or not. But when a sale seemed to be in prospect, they woke speedily to life, and then ensued a scene of haggling and bargaining in which voices rose to screams, and it seemed as though a violent quarrel were going on.

"There won't be any bloodshed," remarked Teddy, grinning, as Don looked apprehensively at an unusually turbulent scene. "They're the best friends in the world. That's just their way of doing business. The shopkeeper asks five times as much as he expects to get. The customer offers one-fifth of what he expects he'll have to pay. One keeps going lower and the other higher until they finally reach a figure that suits them both. It's all in the game."

Before long the Americans reached the French Residency, which comprised a large area of ground about the handsome building over which floated the flag of France.

Captain Sturdy led the way to a section of the compound where, under the shade of a large roof, stood a number of what looked at a distance like ordinary cars.

"There, Amos, are the cars with which, if I'm

any prophet, we're going to cross the desert to the Hoggar Plateau," he said to the professor, as he came to a stand before three cars that were a little apart from the rest.

"Bless my soul!" exclaimed the professor, as he took a startled look at them. "Do you call those cars? If so, they're the queerest I ever saw."

"Look at the back wheels!" ejaculated Don. "Why, they can't touch the sand at all with that long band of rubber in the way."

"That's just where their merit lies," replied the smiling captain, hugely enjoying the wonderment of his companions. "If the wheels travelled on the sand, they'd sink in where the sand was soft. The sand would slip and shift under the wheels, and it would also clog the engine. Then, too, there are miles of sharp stones that would pierce an ordinary tyre. So the Frenchman who made these cars took a leaf from the tanks and put on this caterpillar tread."

"Suppose we ran out of gas?" put in Don.

"I think we can guard against that," was the reply. "Each of these cars has a barrel in the back that will carry two hundred gallons of gasoline. Then, too, I understand that the French Government, with a view of doing some time just what we propose to do, has established stations about 700 miles apart along the route we're going to traverse, and that these are amply supplied. I guess we'll have no trouble on that score."

"How do these machines happen to be in this out-of-the-way corner of the world, anyway?" asked the professor, in some curiosity.

"They're the first consignment of a lot. Others are to follow," explained Captain Sturdy. "These were sent to try them out as a mode of desert travel and see how they worked. The man in charge told me that he and his mechanics had been trying them out for a month past on desert trips of one or two hundred miles at a time, and that they had fulfilled all expectations. The trial tests are over, and these are for sale. The price is reasonable, and we can swing the deal with the funds we have on hand, if we decide that we'll make the venture."

"It is decided, as far as I am concerned," said the professor calmly.

"What?" cried the captain, scarcely daring to believe his ears, for he had not dreamed of so easy a victory and had steeled himself for an argument.

"You heard me," replied the professor, with a smile.

"Good for your sporting blood, Amos!" exclaimed the captain jubilantly, while Don and Teddy hugged each other and fairly danced with glee. "Here comes the man now who has these cars in charge. Let's clinch the thing at once."

The two men advanced to meet a lithe, bronzed man who was coming towards them, and immediately engaged him in an earnest conversation.

The boys, left to themselves for a time, examined the cars with the keenest zest and animation.

"I hope they let me drive one of them!" exclaimed Don.

"Do you know how to drive?" asked Teddy.

"Sure thing," returned Don. "At home I spent most of my spare time about our garage, and our chauffeur taught me about all there was to know about a car. I've helped him take one apart and put it together again until I knew it like a book. Of course, I was too young to get a licence to drive, but when we've been out on lonely country roads, I've been allowed to take the wheel and learn all about running it. Both my uncles are experts in handling a car, so without any extra help at all we could handle these three machines."

"Will you teach me?" asked Teddy eagerly.

"Of course I will, Teddy."

"Call me Brick," said Teddy. "That's the name all the fellows at home used to call me, I suppose on account of the colour of my mop. Somehow it sounds more natural and homelike. It reminds me of America."

"All right," replied Don with a laugh, "Brick it is, then. And you certainly were a perfect brick the way you stood off those two rascals yesterday."

"That's funny!" exclaimed Brick, with a sudden start.

"What's funny?" asked Don, in some surprise, as he looked about him.

"That you should be speaking of those thieves at just the moment they turned up," answered Brick. "There they go now!" and he pointed to two figures hastily disappearing around a corner of the compound.

CHAPTER VII

THE FIGHT FOR MASTERY

"You must be dreaming, Brick," said Don, after a fleeting glimpse of the men as they disappeared.

"Dreaming nothing," was the reply. "I caught a good sight of the face of one of them and I'm sure he was one of the would-be robbers. He had a scar on his left cheek that I noticed yesterday when he was struggling with me. I'm not so dead sure of the other one, but he's probably the same companion that was with the scarred man before. They, likely enough, are pals."

"What do you suppose they were doing around here?" asked Don. "Do you think they're still after that watch of yours?"

"Maybe so," replied Brick. "Perhaps they feel it's hard to let it go when they so nearly had it. More likely, though, they just happened to be here at the same time we were."

"Suppose we follow them and see where they hang out?" suggested Don. "Then we could give the tip to the police and have them arrested."

"All right," assented Brick. "They haven't got much of a start on us."

The boys raced to the place where the men had disappeared and saw them making off rapidly in the direction of the native quarter.

"I know a short cut that will bring us in ahead

of them," said Brick. "Then perhaps we can shadow them when they come along, see where they turn in, and perhaps find out who they are."

The boys were soon in one of the narrow streets with which Brick had become familiar during his stay with Alam, and, peering cautiously around a corner, saw the men approaching.

The boys slipped into one of the bazaars and pretended to be examining goods with an eye to a purchase until the men had passed, and then they followed at a little distance, taking advantage of whatever cover offered until they saw their quarry disappear into a dark lane lined with shabby houses.

They hurried to the entrance of the lane just as the men were disappearing around the farther corner. But when they reached that point all trace was lost.

Brick went in one direction and Don in another, and they hunted about until they became convinced that their search was fruitless.

"No use," sighed Brick disappointedly. "We'll have to let them go for the time. But we'll keep our eyes open for any further tricks they may be trying to play on us."

The boys went back to the compound and turned again to the cars, which had for them an inexhaustible fascination. Up to the present they had been engrossed with the machinery and the odd caterpillar traction feature. Now they noted that on the sides of the cars were brilliant paintings of various kinds of animals and insects. There were a gold beetle, a tortoise, the bull Apis and a crawling caterpillar, besides silver crescents and similar fanciful figures.

"Looks almost like a circus wagon," declared Brick. "I wonder what all the decoration is for."

"I don't know," confessed Don, "but I suppose it is decked out that way so as to strike the fancy of the natives. It will interest them so that our coming among them will make it something like a holiday for them, and it may make them kindly disposed towards us."

"And look at these searchlights!" exclaimed Brick, pointing to especially powerful lights with brilliant reflectors. "They're really humdingers."

"They're dandies all right," agreed Don. He turned one on and was almost startled by the intense beam that leaped forth. "With the help of those we could travel almost as well by night as by day."

"That's lucky," said Brick. "A good deal of travelling will have to be done by night. I know we did when I went with my father——"

His voice trembled here, and he hastily checked himself. Don pretended not to notice, but his own heart ached in sympathy with that of his companion. His own eyes were moist, but he choked back his emotion as he saw that his uncles had concluded their talk with the man who had the cars in charge, and were coming towards him.

"Well, Don," was the captain's cheery salutation, "I guess we can call it a go. We've made our bargain, and to-morrow the cars will be ours."

"That's great!" cried Don. "When can we start?"

"Hold your horses," laughed the captain. "Or rather, since we're talking of cars, put on the brakes. This isn't a matter of simply climbing into the driver's seat, starting the engine and letting in the clutch. We've got to make careful preparations, get in our supplies, engage our men, and do lots of other things before we roll out on the desert. Sure you're not sorry we're going?" he asked quizzically. "Getting cold feet or anything like that, now that the die is cast?"

"Not a bit of it," declared Don stoutly. "I'd start to-day if we could."

"Same here," said Brick.

"I know you would," replied the captain. "Trust you young fellows to need brakes rather than spurs. But come along now, for we've got to hurry back to the hotel and get busy. I want to be ready to start within a week at the very latest."

With a last longing look at the cars, which they hated to leave, the boys followed their elders out of the compound.

"The first thing to do is to find Alam Bokaru," said the captain, as they walked along. "I wish, Teddy, you'd see him as soon as you can and remind him that he promised to come and see me to-night."

"Is Alam going with us?" asked Teddy with delight.

"He is if he will," returned the captain. "He wasn't very keen about it last night on account of that superstition of his, but I hope we can talk him over."

"I hope so," said Teddy. "He knows the desert like a book, and he's got the best reputation of any man I know of in this town for honesty. You can depend on every word he says."

"Isn't that Alam now?" broke in Don, pointing to an Arab with a camel in a stretch of sandy ground between the French Residency and the native quarter of the town.

"Sure enough," agreed Teddy, as he looked in the direction indicated. "He's training a camel. That's his usual job when he isn't acting as a guide. Did you ever see how a camel was trained for mounting?" he asked, turning to Don.

"No, but I'd like to," was the reply. "Is it anything like bronco busting?"

"Not so exciting as that," admitted Teddy. "But it takes a lot of skill and patience, and Alam's a dabster at it. Just watch him for a minute."

They drew nearer and watched the performance with interest. The Arab was so engrossed in his task that he had not noticed their approach.

As the first step in the mounting process, Alam was endeavouring to make the camel squat upon the ground. The beast had his own views on that subject, however, and resolutely refused, rearing and pulling violently against the rope that was attached to his nostrils, while the other end was held in the hand of the trainer. For some minutes the struggle continued, and it seemed as though Alam's arm would be wrenched from its socket. But those arm muscles were like tempered steel, and the man held on to the rope with a grip like that of death.

But strength was not the only requisite, or even the main one. All the time that the struggle persisted, Alam kept crooning to the beast in a chanting monotone, like a mother soothing a restless babe.

"What's he doing that for?" Don asked.

"He's sort of hypnotising it, I guess," explained

Brick. "Something like an Indian serpent charmer when he chants to his snakes or plays some musical instrument. See, it's beginning to work."

The resistance of the camel was sensibly weakening, and gradually, with many grunts of enraged protest, his knees began to bend and he finally sank to the ground.

With lightning-like quickness, Alam threw on a saddle and adjusted the reins. Then he seized the reins in his right hand and placed that hand on the front of the saddle. At the same time, he seized the camel's nostrils in his left hand and turned the brute's head inward until the nose nearly touched the front of the saddle. Then the trainer rapidly threw his right leg over the saddle and placed his left foot on the camel's neck. The beast leaped upwards with a disconcerting jerk, and here it was that Alam's mastery of the situation was put to the test.

With a quickness surprising in so clumsy a beast, the camel thrust his head and body backwards and forwards with tremendous violence, so that it seemed inevitable that the rider should be unseated and hurled to the ground.

But Alam countered by rapidly jerking his body in the inverse direction, timing every action like a flash so as to counteract each movement of the angry brute as soon as it was made. It was a superb exhibition of strategy and nerve, and the breathless spectators had all they could do to keep from applauding. They refrained, however, lest it should distract the rider's attention from the difficult task he had on hand.

For perhaps ten minutes the fight continued, and then the camel gave in and acknowledged that he had met his master. Alam dismounted, gave the beast an amicable pat on the neck, and then for the first time noted the group of onlookers. He came towards them with a smile and a low bow.

"Good work, Alam Bokaru," commended the professor, in the Arab's native tongue. "It is not for naught that you are called the master of camels."

A momentary light in the Arab's eyes showed that he was pleased with the compliment, but his features retained their customary immobility.

"All skill in man is the gift of Allah," was the noncommittal reply he vouchsafed.

"I am glad we met you," remarked the captain. "We were just asking Teddy to look you up and remind you that you were to come to the hotel to-night. Perhaps you can go along with us now."

"I will tether the camel and come," Alam said.

He secured the animal, and then joined the party and accompanied them to the hotel.

"Now, Alam," said the professor, when they had seated themselves in the suite occupied by them, "we've settled the matter that we were talking about last night. We're going into the Sahara Desert, as far at least as the Hoggar Plateau."

The Arab inclined his head.

"The white man does as he will," he replied.

"But we want you to come along," the professor continued, while Don and Brick eagerly watched Alam's face to see how he received the proposition.

"To look upon the City of Brass is death," intoned Alam.

"What a single track mind the man has," muttered the captain to himself.

"Only if he sees it from the back of a camel," said the professor patiently.

"So it is written," agreed the master of camels.

"If you see it at all, it won't be from a camel's back," asserted the professor.

"How else, in the desert?" asked Alam in wonder.

"We're not going to take any camels along," was the reply. "We're going with cars."

For an instant the Arab was moved from his usual calm. It could plainly be seen that the thought was revolutionary. Perhaps it struck him as impious. For a few moments, as he pondered the problem, there was silence.

"Why then do you want Alam Bokaru?" he asked, after a brief space. "He cannot drive a car. He is a master of camels."

"He's weakening," whispered Brick, giving Don a jubilant nudge in the ribs.

"We want you," replied the professor, "because you know the desert better than any man in Tuggurt. We want you because we believe you to be honest, courageous and straightforward. We want you because we believe that with you we have the best chance to discover and rescue Mr. Allison. You are fond of Teddy. You saved his life. Now help him to get back his father."

"Amos has struck the right chord," muttered the captain to himself, as he watched the Arab narrowly.

That a conflict was going on in Alam's mind was apparent. On the one hand was his ingrained dread and suspicion of anything new, anything that deviated from the beaten track that his ancestors had trodden for generations. On the other was his real affection for the boy he had rescued and the chance that he might give that boy something that he would regard as priceless. Perhaps, too, there was a certain fascination in the new and untried adventure that appealed to this courageous man of the desert accustomed, as he was, to taking chances.

At last he reached a decision. He bowed to the floor three times in the direction of the east, as though committing his affairs into the hands of Allah. Then he rose to his feet and drew his robes about him with a certain instinctive grace and dignity.

"I will go," he said.

CHAPTER VIII

INTO THE DESERT WASTES

AT Alam Bokaru's words there was a shout of delight from Don and Brick and a look of intense gratification on the faces of Captain Sturdy and Professor Bruce.

"Good for you, Alam!" exclaimed the captain, extending his hand. "As far as it is in our power, we'll see that you never regret it. And now, let's get down to business. There's no end of things to be done and very little time to do them in."

There followed a long and earnest conversation on ways and means, in which Alam's knowledge and long experience proved to be invaluable.

The party already consisted of five persons, and as they had but three cars, each of which would have to be heavily loaded with oil, gasoline and supplies, it was desirable to limit the number who should go along as much as possible.

It was finally decided to take one other man, which would give two people to each car. Alam suggested a cousin of his, Abdullah by name, whom he recommended as brave and trustworthy. It was agreed that he should form one of the party.

The cars were to be driven by the captain, the professor and Don respectively. The latter was very young for the work, but both of his uncles knew that he could drive well, and they also had confidence in his coolness, courage and marksmanship, though they hoped that there would be no call for a display of the latter accomplishment.

An ample supply of firearms and ammunition was arranged for, however, in case of emergency. Alam himself was a much better shot than the average Arab. A couple of machine guns were to be taken along, and these, with their rain of bullets, would immensely increase the strength of the expedition. But it was agreed beforehand that there would be no use made of any weapon unless it became absolutely necessary to defend their lives. Both the captain and the professor had had many dealings with natives quite as wild as any with whom they were likely to be brought in contact, and their diplomacy had usually been sufficient for any situation that arose.

The captain was to lead the way in the first car, with Alam as his companion. Don and Brick were to follow in the second, and the professor and Abdullah were to bring up the rear in the third. In this way, the boys, in case danger threatened, would have reinforcements in front and back, and could thus be guarded against any surprise attack.

The providing of the food supplies was arranged for largely by Don's uncles themselves; but Alam took it upon himself to suggest other things indispensable for a desert journey.

The guerba, or water skin, almost invariably used by the nomads was discarded, because of the inevitable loss by leakage, which in a long journey often proved a serious matter. In place of these, it was determined to use aluminium cylindrical vessels that could not burst and which would preserve the water to the last drop.

But there were the mesoueds, or leathern bags, to hold the supplies, the delous, or water buckets, also made of leather, and the long ropes of hide necessary to draw the water from the wells, some of which in the desert were more than three hundred feet in depth. All of these and a host of other necessities were suggested by Alam, and again and again Don's uncles had reason to congratulate themselves on having secured for the expedition a guide so experienced and wise in desert needs.

They did not have to bother about tents, for these were already part of the cars' equipment, one being rolled up on the side of each car. These could readily be set up with the aid of a few stout poles.

During the busy days that followed, the boys, as well as their elders, found their hands full in attending to errands in various quarters of the town.

Brick proved of special value in this regard, as he had a sufficient smattering of the Arab tongue to make himself fairly well understood by the tradesmen, and he also knew enough of their cunning methods of bargaining not to be taken in.

One day, when the lads had been unusually busy for an hour or two and were hot and perspiring, they sat down on the sands in the shadow of the side of one of the little shops, the front of which faced the adjoining street.

"Uncle Frank said this morning that we would be ready to start day after to-morrow," remarked Don.

"Can't get off too soon," replied Brick. "I'm just crazy to take up the hunt for my father. There isn't a night now that I don't dream about him."

"I know just how you feel about it," said Don sympathetically, as he thought of the many nights when he had had a similar dream of his missing father, mother and sister. "If we can only find your father alive and well and get him away from the Arabs, it won't matter much whether we do the other things or not."

"It's awfully good of you to feel that way," responded Brick. "Just the same, I hope you find the other things you're after, too. Your Uncle Frank would be mightily disappointed if he didn't find the Cave of Emeralds."

"Do you really think there is a Cave of Emeralds?" asked Don, with a slight touch of scepticism in his tone that was not lost on his companion.

"I'm sure there is," declared Teddy stoutly. "My

father had studied up the matter and he hadn't the least doubt about it."

"I wonder what the treasure will amount to, if we do find it," remarked Don.

"I shouldn't wonder if it might be hundreds of thousands of dollars," said Brick.

"Hundreds of thousands!" gasped Don. "Go on, you're kidding me!"

"Honest Injun, no!" cried Brick. "It wouldn't take more than a handful or two of emeralds to amount to that. Father was sure that if he found the Cave of Emeralds it would make him rich for life."

"I wish we were out there in the desert now looking for it," said Don, his imagination fired by the prospect.

"Only a little while to wait now."

"What's that noise " asked Don suddenly.

"I don't hear any noise."

"Sounded like a shuffling or a rustling." Don jumped to his feet and stepped briskly to the corner.

He was just in time to see several Arabs of the rougher sort scurrying into an alley on the farther side of the building. There was an undeniable air of haste about them, as though they were anxious to escape discovery. The face of one of them, he noticed, was marked by a scar.

He hurried after them, but by the time he got to the entrance of the alley no one was in sight. The group had vanished as completely as though the earth had opened up and swallowed them. With a vague sense of uneasiness, he retraced his steps and rejoined his companion.

"What was it?" asked Brick quickly, as he noted the perturbed countenance of his friend.

"There was a bunch of Arabs there that seemed to have been snooping around and listening," answered Don.

"I wonder if they were," mused Brick, catching something of the apprehension that Don betrayed.

"There seems to have been no other reason for their disappearing in such a hurry when they heard me coming," was the reply. "I tell you, Brick, we made a mistake by talking about those emeralds in a place where we might be overheard."

"It was careless of us, for a fact," admitted Brick. "But probably nothing will come of it. We didn't mention the district in which the Cave of Emeralds is supposed to lie."

"No; but we did say that we were going to look for them," replied Don, "and all those fellows would have to do would be to get a lot of rascals together and try to follow us or ambush us."

"Oh, I guess it won't come to anything like that," affirmed Brick, though he was far from feeling as confident as his words implied.

"At any rate, I'm going to tell my uncles all about it," Don declared. "I hate to admit I've been so imprudent, but they ought to be put on their guard in case there should be any mischief brewing."

He was as good as his word, and narrated the incident the moment he got back to the hotel. The professor was inclined to be a little grave, but the captain made light of it.

"Probably just a bunch of lazy Algerians, listening, if they listened at all, just out of curiosity," he said, with a wave of his hand. "Probably by this time, even if they were able to make head or tail of it, they've forgotten all about the matter. At any rate, they'd have their work cut out for them, if they tried to follow us. We'd make five miles in the cars while they were making one with their camels. I guess we won't have to worry about them, although I'm glad you told us, Don, and we'll keep it in mind."

Two days later, the party was ready to start. The cars were thoroughly equipped with all the supplies needed. They had been gone over with the utmost care to see that they were in perfect condition and they had been tried out by Don and his uncles over a twenty-mile stretch of the desert. All were delighted at the ease with which they negotiated the obstacles that were a fair sample of any others they would be likely to encounter on their journey.

They left Tuggurt just at dawn. Despite the early hour, a large number of the French officials of the town were on hand to see them off and wish them good luck. There was quite a large gathering of natives, too, for, outside of the matter of the emeralds, there had been no attempt, which would have been fruitless in any event, to keep the projected expedition secret.

Abdullah, the cousin of Alam, had turned up, and was in the last car with the professor. He was a stalwart, clean-cut young fellow, and the party had taken a liking to him at once. As Don and Brick were seated in the second car, waiting for the word, Don's eye fell upon the face of a native in the fringe of the crowd. He nudged his companion.

"See who's here!" he exclaimed. "The man with the scar! The same one you think tried to rob you and the same that I saw slinking into the alley the day we were talking about the emeralds."

"Sure thing," agreed Brick, as he singled out the man Don indicated. "Same old rascal turning up like a bad penny. Villainous face he has, all right."

"I wish I knew just what thoughts are going on behind that face."

"Regret that he didn't get my watch probably."

"Or plans perhaps to rob the bunch of us on a good deal bigger scale," muttered Don, thinking of his unlucky slip on the question of the emeralds.

"Let him catch us," laughed Brick. "He'd have his work cut out for him. It would be like a tortoise trying to catch a hare."

"True enough," assented Don. "But that wouldn't stop him and his gang from laying for us on the way back."

"That's right! I never thought of that."

At that moment the boys' thoughts were taken off that unpleasant subject by the agreed-upon signal for starting, three loud blasts from the horn of the leading car. Don threw in the clutch, the captain and professor did the same, and the cars started forward, while a shout went up from the crowd.

"We're off!" shouted Don, as he eased the car into its stride, accommodating his pace to that of the captain's car in front.

"Off!" echoed Brick, his pulses throbbing with excitement. "Off to the desert! Off to find my father!"

CHAPTER IX

DESPITE the heavy loads that the cars carried, they moved along with gratifying speed. There was no attempt to let them out to the limit, as safety was the watchword. There would be plenty of time for speeding if there should be need for haste, after the drivers had learned what they could do with the cars and had become familiar with the character of the going.

In the immediate vicinity of Tuggurt, the sand in many places was loose and shifting. But before long the travellers came to a region where the sand was as smooth and almost as hard as a floor, so hard indeed that as they looked behind them, they could scarcely detect any trace of their passage.

"Nothing the matter with this as a road," exulted Brick. "Why, it's almost as good as a speedway track. It's like some of those Florida beaches you read about, where they hold car races."

"Don't crow too soon," counselled Don, as he devoted all his attention to the steering. "This is velvet all right, but there'll be plenty of tough places to make up for it."

He spoke with some difficulty, for he had not yet become accustomed to the litham that he wore. This was a thin blue veil that covered almost all his face except his eyes, the latter being protected by huge blue sun glasses. The litham is an absolute necessity to prevent the wearer being choked by the clouds of sand that are constantly blowing about the Sahara. Then, too, Alam had told them that the use of it prevented thirst to a remarkable extent.

"Gee," chuckled Brick, who was similarly accoutred, "we must look like something that the cat dragged in."

"I guess we do," laughed Don, as he gave the wheel a twist and cleverly avoided a hillock. "Neither one of us would take a prize in a beauty show."

Before long, the town of Tuggurt vanished below the horizon. Its disappearance seemed to mark the severance of all ties with civilisation. All about them nothing was to be seen but desert, an apparently boundless ocean of sand, compared with whose immensity the three cars seemed like so many black ants creeping over its surface.

The sun was like a ball of burnished brass in a cloudless sky as it came up from the east and flung its fierce rays on the sand beneath. The ground shimmered with the heat waves that rose quiveringly above it and wrapped themselves about the travellers.

"It's lucky that we can make our own breeze as we go along," remarked Brick.

"That will be one incentive to make good time," replied Don. "The faster we go, the better the breeze. Though we've got to admit that the breeze doesn't bring much refreshment with it. It feels as though it came from the mouth of a fiery furnace."

A little to one side of the path they traversed they noted a collection of bones and skulls of camels.

"Alam says the whole desert is strewn with them," remarked Brick, as their glances met. "Sometimes they just give out and die in their tracks. At other times, a whole caravan is overwhelmed by a sandstorm."

The sight sobered the boys a little, and gave them some idea of the perils that attended the journey on which they had embarked. It was full of romance, to be sure, but also full of danger. Just as the floor of the sea was strewn with wrecks, so this ocean of sand had many times claimed the lives of those who defied it.

"Oh, for a drink of water!" murmured Brick, as he passed his tongue over his dry lips. "Now's the time that I envy the camels who can go a week on a stretch without it."

"We'll have to get used to being thirsty," rejoined Don. "But that will make the water all the more refreshing when it comes. That won't be long now, for Uncle Frank said that we'd stop and pitch camp after we'd been riding for a couple of hours."

"We'll have to camp right in the open," remarked Teddy, as his eyes roved over the boundless plain that lay baking in the sun, with not a tree to break the monotony all the way to the skyline.

"The tents will give us shelter enough from the sun," replied Don. "Then, too, the cars themselves will cast a shadow, and we can follow the shadow around, and so get the best of old Sol."

But those in the party were game, and whatever

discomfort they experienced they took as all in the day's work. The novelty of the situation atoned to a great extent for whatever unpleasant features accompanied it. They had not come on a holiday jaunt, but had embarked on a great adventure, and they were willing to pay the cost.

What secrets did the desert hold? How many of those secrets was it going to yield up to them? These were the questions that made their blood tingle with eager anticipation.

The sun had mounted high in the heavens when the leading car slowed up and a loud blast from its horn signalled for a halt.

Don turned off the engine and came to within a few feet of the captain's car where he stopped, being joined in a moment more by the rearguard machine driven by the professor.

All jumped out and stretched their limbs, grateful for the release from their cramped position, while Alam and Abdullah, with the dexterity born of long practice, unrolled the tents and set them up, sheltered by the cars as much as possible from the fierceness of the sun.

"Well, Don, how do you like your first taste of driving in the desert?" asked the captain, as he threw his arm affectionately over his nephew's shoulder.

"First rate," was the quiet reply. "Though I'd like the taste of something else still better."

"Meaning water, I suppose," replied the captain. "I guess you're not alone in that. Just now you can have all you want, for there are good wells at Wargla, and we can fill the tanks again. You'll find it rather warm, but you won't mind a little thing like that."

He took some cups out of their kit, filled them from one of the aluminium tanks, and passed them around. The water was warm, as he had predicted, but to their parched throats it tasted like nectar. They drank and drank until they could drink no more.

"And now for a little grub," said the captain. "That is," he added, with a twinkle in his eye as he looked at the boys, "if you don't object."

"Object!" cried Brick. "Lead me to it."

"The only thing I object to is the word ' little.'" And Don grinned as he settled himself on the sand.

Sandwiches were handed out to begin with, and they ate them with avidity. The captain opened some canned goods that provided an abundant meal.

"All the comforts of home," murmured Don, when at last he had satisfied his clamorous appetite.

"Not quite," objected the professor. "I could do without some of this sand that goes with every mouthful."

"That's part of the menu in the desert," affirmed the captain. "The sand sifts in everywhere. The very air is full of minute particles of it. We'll breathe and we'll eat it until we get back to civilisation. But the Arabs seem to thrive on it, and I guess it won't hurt us. They say, anyhow, that everybody has to eat a peck of dirt during his life. Here's where we get our peck."

"How long do we camp here?" asked Don.

"Until about five this afternoon," was the reply. "Until we get used to the heat, it would be simply suicide to try to travel in the middle of the day. The moon rises early to-night, and we can do a good deal of travelling by its light. If we have luck, we'll get to Wargla, our first stop, by nine or ten o'clock."

"In the meantime," suggested the professor, "it would be well to get as much sleep as possible. We can get some of the blankets from the cars and use them as pillows."

"Seems odd to talk of blankets in this oven of a place," laughed Don.

"There'll be plenty of times when we'll be mighty glad to have them," replied the professor. "When the weather gets down to zero, we'll bless our stars that we brought them along."

"Zero!" exclaimed Brick incredulously. "In this desert?"

"Just so," was the rejoinder. "We'll feel many a bitterly cold blast before we get out of here. Sometimes the thermometer drops sixty points in an hour."

They stretched out and slept soundly for hours, and the sun was well on its way to the western horizon when they opened their eyes. The heat was sensibly abating, and they moved about with renewed vigour, enormously refreshed by the intermission.

The road still continued hard and good. Every mile of such travelling they regarded as clear gain, or, as Brick phrased it, "velvet," for they well knew that there were many stretches to be encountered that would test all their own skill and the strength and endurance of their cars.

They journeyed over vast expanses strewn with little brown and yellow pebbles, glistening like gems in the rays of the sun. Just before dark a small caravan passed them, coming from the other direction. That the desert nomads were greatly excited and impressed by the sight of the cars was evident by the suddenness with which they came to a halt, talking wildly and vociferously among themselves and pointing to the strange invaders of a domain that hitherto had belonged to them alone. But the cars plunged along without stopping, though their inmates waved their hands in friendly fashion to the Arabs, and soon the caravan was lost to sight.

Darkness came suddenly, and it was now that the searchlights with which the cars were provided stood the drivers in good stead, flinging their powerful beams into the night and lighting up the way for a long distance ahead.

Soon, however, these became unnecessary, for, as the captain had remarked, the moon rose early and flooded the vast expanse with splendour. Then the Americans saw the desert under a new and witching guise. The scene was beautiful beyond description. The sand under the brilliant rays of the moon looked like a white sheet. All the aridity of the landscape was transformed by the dazzling sheen into fairyland. It was as though the travellers were voyaging in another sphere. The strange effect was heightened by the silence that enveloped them, broken only by the chugging of the cars as they ploughed along.

The spell was broken by an exclamation from Brick.

"Look!" he said eagerly, putting his hand on Don's arm. "See those lights. We're coming to a town."

In the distance gleamed a multitude of tiny lights that told of human habitations.

"Good!" ejaculated Don. "I guessed we must be near it. I just saw from the speedometer that we had nearly covered the hundred and twenty-five miles that lie between Wargla and Tuggurt. Pretty good work for the first day, considering how much time we spent in resting."

They were descending now, for the town of Wargla that they were approaching lay in a low basin, surrounded by sand hills. They soon reached the outskirts and quickly made their way to the French Residency, a spacious, handsome building, very similar to the one in Tuggurt. There was no hotel in the town, but they received a hearty welcome from the French Resident and his staff, who had been apprised of their coming and had extended an invitation to the party to be their guests during their stay.

A bountiful repast had been prepared for them, and their hosts outdid themselves in their hospitality. What the travellers enjoyed most of all was the cold bath with which they regaled themselves before retiring to their rooms. Never before had one been so grateful, the more so because they knew that probably many days would pass before they could expect to have another.

But quite as important as food and bath to the

professor, was the opportunity he found at the post to add to his collection. There was a large aggregation of minerals in the desert, secured by the officers from the caravans that passed through the place. Rare curios, specimens of ancient pottery, brass-work, weapons, gathered from the ruins of cities that once had flourished in that vast expanse, were there in abundance.

The American had expected to leave the next morning, but some minor troubles had developed with the cars, and it was necessary that repairs be made before they again ventured into the desert. These occupied the major part of the morning.

Shortly before noon, Don and Brick sallied forth into one of the date groves for which the place was famous. The shadow of the trees furnished a soothing refuge from the heat, and the fruit itself, fresh from the trees, was delicious.

They sat down under one of the date palms, Brick with his back against the tree and Don near him, idly toying with a stick he had picked up from the ground.

Suddenly Don saw something on a little projection of the tree directly over Brick's head that made him give a quick start.

"What's the matter?" asked Brick, noting the intent look on his friend's face. This look slowly turned to one of horror.

"Don't move, Brick!" came the tense warning. "Don't move—for your life, don't move!"

CHAPTER X

A NARROW ESCAPE

STARTLED as he was by Don's ominous command, Brick managed to get sufficient control of his muscles to obey and remained as he was, absolutely without movement. He dared not look up, and had not the slightest idea of what menaced him.

But Don saw and realised it to the full. Not more than six inches from Brick's head was a huge tarantula. Its eight eyes were focused on Brick's neck and the repulsive, hairy body was already flattened for a spring. The horrible creature was the very image of malignity.

Slowly, for fear of angering the tarantula and precipitating the tragedy that seemed so dreadfully near, Don raised the stick he was holding high above his head. Then with a movement like lightning he struck.

Fortunately, his aim was true, and he caught the hideous thing full and fair. It fell to the ground in a mangled mass, its horrible falces quivering convulsively, but now forever beyond the possibility of doing harm.

Brick shuddered and jumped to his feet as the creature fell beside him, almost brushing him as it passed.

"All right now, Brick!" exclaimed Don, with a voice somewhat broken, now that the strain had passed. "A second more though, and that thing would have been on your throat."

"And from what I've heard of them, that would probably have been the end of me," gasped Teddy, as he kicked the still writhing object out of reach and viewed it with a sense of sickening repulsion. "Don, I don't know how to thank you enough. That's the second time you've proved a mighty good friend in need."

"It was just luck that I saw it when I did," replied Don. "Luck, too, that I had this good stick in my hand."

"But it was pluck, not luck, that made you keep your nerve and smash the creature," replied Brick. "Lots of fellows would have been too scared to do anything. But let's get away from here. There may be other little playfellows like that around, and one is enough for a morning."

"Right you are!" exclaimed Don, as with a shiver of disgust he perceived another of the swollen, ugly creatures crawling far up the trunk of the tree.

"Look out!" screamed Brick.

Don dodged, but as he drew back he felt something hairy graze his cheek.

A tarantula had sprung, but Brick's warning and Don's quickness had made it miss its mark. It fell to the ground, and before it could renew the attack, Brick's heel had crushed it.

That was enough for the boys, and they stood not on the order of their going but went at once.

The repairs were completed, the water tanks filled, and their supply of gasoline replenished shortly after noon. As they were anxious to be on their way, they left Wargla about five o'clock in the afternoon, despite the cordial urging of their hosts to stay over another day.

They had driven for perhaps an hour when they came to a little oasis in the desert where lived an influential Arab chief. He himself, with some of his tribe, had seen the coming of the party from afar and had come out to the edge of the oasis, making signals of friendship and welcome.

As it was the policy of Don's uncles to gain, wherever possible, the goodwill of the nomads, the captain stopped his car when he came near the chief. The other cars drew up alongside.

The chief bowed low and spoke some words that were evidently in the nature of an invitation.

"What is it he is saying, Alam?" the captain asked of the master of camels.

"He tells us that a meal is ready," answered Alam, "and asks us to stop and partake of it with him."

The captain turned in some perplexity to the professor.

"What do you think, Amos?" he asked. "He seems a friendly fellow, and I don't want to antagonise him. Yet I hate like the mischief to lose time."

"I think it would be policy to accept the invitation," replied the professor. "When you're in Rome, you know, do as the Romans do. We've got to conform to the customs of the country. He'd feel hurt if we refused his invitation and consider that we'd insulted him. It's just touch and go whether we make of him a friend or an enemy, and we can't have too many friends in the desert."

The good sense of this was apparent, and as the boys also were eager to have a new experience and Alam, too, thought it expedient to comply, they accepted the invitation with thanks, and were led to the chief's house, a low one-storied dwelling.

Their hearts misgave them though, when they saw the nature of the feast provided. There were several huge dishes of oily looking food, the nature of which could only be guessed at. The apartment was intolerably hot, and the flies settled over everything in swarms.

"I guess we're in for it," whispered Brick to Don.

"Looks like it," was the reply. "But we can only die once, and we'll have to go through with it."

One dish looked less uninviting than the others. It consisted of rice with spices.

"I'm going to take a stab at that," remarked Don.

But he was mistaken if he thought he was going to be let off so easily. A low warning from Alam, passed around among the party, told them that they were expected to partake of everything that was on the table. Moreover, if they took only a small portion, some hospitably inclined subject of the chief was sure to heap their plate. It was one of the most trying ordeals through which they had ever passed, but they summoned up all their resolution and made martyrs of themselves for fear of offending their host.

At last most of the eatables had been disposed of, and they drew a sigh of relief.

"So far, so bad," murmured Don to Brick.

"Never again," vouchsafed Brick fervently.

But they discovered that there was more to come,

and Don stifled a groan when a whole sheep, roasted, was produced and set with a flourish of pride on the table. This was evidently the main dish of the feast. It was prepared in strange fashion with much oil, of which they were already sick, and covered with chili peppers.

"Such a mess!" shuddered Brick.

"We've gone so far we'll have to go a little farther," said Don, summoning up all his fortitude.

They worried through the feast as best they could, their repulsion not diminished by the manner of eating of their hosts. The chief ate with great gusto, smacking his lips and tossing pieces to his followers, of whom there were about a dozen present, who bolted them like so many wolves. It was evidently regarded by them as a gala occasion, and they made the most of it.

It was an enormous relief to the Americans when at last the repast was finished and, after elaborate thanks to their well-meaning host, they adjourned to the open air.

Here again, although they were impatient to be off, they had to wait for another half-hour while the chief and his followers gathered about the car and examined with childish delight the brightly coloured symbols painted on the sides. But their pleasure passed all bounds when the captain passed around some trinkets that he had brought along especially for that purpose.

Finally the compliments and bowings came to an end and the party climbed into the cars and were off, hooting their horns in farewell to the waving hands of their hosts.

"Well, that's that," remarked Don, as he threw in the clutch. "My curiosity as to Arab meals has been fully satisfied. If we don't die of acute indigestion, we'll be lucky."

"It was tough," agreed Brick, who had not suffered as much as the rest, because, from living with Alam, he had become somewhat accustomed to Arabian cookery. "But, at any rate, we've made a friend. We don't know at what time his friendship may come in handy."

The route they were now following was that of an old watercourse, known as the Wady Mia. The country was rougher than it had been at the start. The expanse of sand was dotted with dried shrubs and clumps of grasses, which, as Alam explained, made excellent food for camels, but made it much more difficult for car travelling.

This was compensated for somewhat, however, by the fact that the old watercourse furnished a landmark, and by following its outline they knew they were going in the right direction.

"Seems queer to think that there was once a rushing river along this old dried-up bed," remarked Brick.

"It sure does," agreed Don. "I'd give a good deal to see some water in there now. We could get plenty to drink, and then, too, we could take a bath whenever we wanted to. Uncle Amos says that at one time the whole Sahara was a place of rivers and lakes and farms and orchards, one of the most beautiful and fertile places in the world. And what is more, he says it may be again. There's plenty of water deep down underneath the sand, and the

French have already dug dozens of artesian wells and are planning to have a chain of them all over the desert."

"Sounds like a dream," said Brick.

"Maybe so," agreed Don. "But science these days is making lots of dreams come true."

The moon rose, and some of the mystery and enchantment of the night before descended upon them. It was almost as light as day, and the drivers had no trouble in keeping up the speed of their cars. But this day all had been without sleep, and they were more tired than usual when the horn of the captain's car sounded the signal for a halt.

"What's that?" asked Brick, after he and Don had climbed out of their car, pointing to something that sparkled silvery white in the moonlight.

Don gave one look and bounded towards it.

CHAPTER XI

IN PERIL OF THEIR LIVES

"It's water!" cried Don, as he reached a little rock from which the water was falling in a steady stream with a tinkling, musical sound. He laved his hot face and hands with it. "Water coming from the rock!"

"Like the rock smitten by Moses," said the professor, with a smile. "An unusual sight in the desert, and, as a matter of fact, the only one of its kind within eight hundred miles. Use all you like of it, boys, either for drinking or bathing. It's probably been running for hundreds of years, and it isn't going to stop now."

The boys needed no urging, and their example was followed by the rest of the party. The water was delightfully cool in contrast to the water in their tanks, which had been heated by the desert journey and which, though it supplied their actual physical needs, brought with it little sense of refreshment. They drank till they could drink no more.

"Did you know that we were coming to this?" asked Don, a little later, as they were resting, while Alam and Abdullah prepared their tents and beds for the night.

"Yes," replied the smiling captain. "But I kept quiet about it because I wanted you to have a little surprise. Not an unpleasant one, was it?"

"You bet it wasn't!" cried Don, and Brick echoed him.

"Alam was telling me about it as we came along," continued Don's uncle. "He says that when he is travelling as guide to a caravan he times the stages of a journey so as to spend a night here."

Cooled and refreshed, all slept well that night, and when the Americans were awakened by Alam at dawn they felt in fine fettle for the work of the day.

Having drunk their fill of the cooling water of the spring and replenished their tanks, they started, with a regretful look behind at the trickling stream that had contributed so greatly to their comfort, and whose like they had no expectation of meeting again.

They made the most of the early hours, and had covered a good distance before they stopped at about ten o'clock to rest until the day grew cooler. The Americans were preparing to take a nap when a sudden exclamation of Alam called them to the openings of their tents.

Coming towards them at a rapid gait was a group of wild-looking nomads mounted on camels. All of them were armed with rifles. This was not in itself alarming, as everybody goes armed in the desert. But there was something sinister and aggressive in their appearance and actions that at once aroused suspicion.

"Get your guns," commanded the captain, as he took his own rifle in the hollow of his arm and stepped outside the tent.

"What do you make of them, Alam?" he asked of the guide, who was studying keenly the coming riders, eight in number.

"They are robbers," pronounced Alam, as he got his own weapon in readiness.

The boys were tense with excitement and their hearts were beating rapidly. Don's eyes blazed as he looked over his rifle and slipped a cartridge into the breech. Brick also was armed, though he was not specially proficient in the use of a weapon. But his heart was in the right place, and at close quarters, as this struggle promised to be, if it really materialised, he would have to be reckoned with.

As the riders drew nearer, it could be seen that they were well armed. Each man had an almost new carbine with a bandolier full of ammunition slung beside it. In addition every one had at his saddle two swords and a spear.

"Get behind the cars and don't fire unless I give the word," commanded the captain, though he himself stepped out into the open, accompanied by Alam.

The leader of the newcomers was a stalwart man. He wore a vivid red cloth thrown over his shoulders and on his legs were leather boots reaching almost to his thigh, into which his baggy trousers had been thrust. The litham covered the greater portion of his face, permitting only a hooked nose like a hawk's and a pair of fierce black eyes to be seen. His followers were less elaborately attired. They were mounted on shaggy-haired camels, which seemed to be built for speed and were in excellent condition.

The fearlessness of the captain in coming forward alone to meet them seemed to impress the Arabs and they checked their speed until they came to a stop about twenty yards away.

With his gaze fixed unwaveringly upon them, Captain Sturdy, followed by the guide, walked towards them until he was within speaking distance.

"Ask them what they want, Alam," commanded the captain.

Alam addressed the leader of the party, who responded curtly.

"He says," translated Alam, turning towards the captain, "that no one passes through this part of the desert without paying him tribute. You must do the same."

"I see," said the captain, with a faintly amused smile. "Ask him what tribute he demands."

Again Alam spoke to the leader.

"He himself will be the judge of that," he reported. "He will search through the devil wagons and take what he and his followers may want. You may keep the rest and go on your way."

"That's good of him," remarked the captain ironically. "Ask him what will happen if we refuse."

"Then you may commit your souls to Allah, for he will kill you all," was Alam's translation of the leader's answer.

"Tell him first," commanded the captain, "to watch the magic of the white man's rifle."

He took from his pocket a small bottle that he had picked up as he passed out of the tent. He held it aloft and made with it a series of passes in the air. The bandits watched him as though hypnotised, their curiosity and superstition aroused by this, to them, mystical movements.

Then, while they watched, he threw the bottle high in the air, put his rifle to his shoulder and fired. The crack of the rifle was followed by the crash of glass, and the fragments of the bottle fell to the sand.

It was splendid markmanship, and it created a sensation among the bandits, who gathered their reins tightly in their hands and looked around as though contemplating flight.

The captain held up his hand.

"Tell the chief," he ordered Alam, "that that is nothing to what the white man can do."

It was evident now that fear, as well as curiosity, held the band intent on Captain Sturdy's next action.

He took from his pocket a silver coin, held it up so that they could see it, made another series of mysterious passes and flung it far from him. His rifle leaped to his shoulder, and the coin, bent and battered fell some distance away.

A shout of surprise and consternation went up from the bandits. What magic was this that the foreigners summoned at will?

The captain took instant advantage of their demoralisation. His whole manner changed. Up to now he had been quiet and restrained. Now his face became terrible. He flung his repeating rifle to his shoulder and swept it like lightning around the huddled circle.

"Go!" he shouted in a voice like thunder. And they went, went like scared rabbits, went in mad panic, crowding upon each other's heels as they spurred their camels on with wild shouts to get out of the range of that death-dealing rifle. The captain lowered his weapon and turned with a grim smile towards the tent, while the others of the party rushed towards him full of admiration.

"Oh, Uncle Frank," cried Don, "you were great, simply great!"

"One of the finest things I ever saw done," declared Amos Bruce earnestly. "We're proud of you, Frank."

"Oh, it was nothing," disclaimed the captain modestly. "I didn't want it to come to a fight, for we'd probably have had to kill some of the rascals, and although they might have deserved killing, I didn't want it to be at our hands. And then, too, some of us might have been hurt. The easiest way in this case proved to be the best way."

"I guess that will hold them for a while," exulted Don.

"I imagine it will," replied the captain. "They won't want any more of our game. We shan't be troubled any more—by that special band, at least. And likely enough they'll spread the news that it's best to leave the men with the devil wagons, as they call them, alone."

There were no further alarms that day nor for days to come, although as a matter of precaution one of the party kept on guard while the others slept.

But other than human enemies were abroad, as they found out before their trip was over. The desert was whining for its prey!

CHAPTER XII

BURIED ALIVE

"I WONDER what's the matter with me," remarked Don, as he woke one morning and sat up in his tent. "I'm tingling all over."

"Same here," said Brick. "Little prickly feeling going over me, and this red hair of mine won't lie down. Keeps standing up on end as though I were scared about something. I wonder what makes it."

"Perhaps it's just excitement," conjectured Don. "Or maybe a little more sand than usual has got inside our clothes."

"It isn't that," remarked Professor Bruce, who in passing the opening of their tent had overheard the conversation. "There's an unusual amount of electricity in the air, as though something were brewing. Probably a storm of some kind is coming up."

"I wish it were a rainstorm," said Don.

"You said it!" observed Brick. "Gee, wouldn't it be great to sit out on the sand and get soaked. Wouldn't catch us putting up umbrellas."

"We may have that experience before we get through," replied the professor. "Sometimes there are rainstorms in the Sahara that are almost like cloudbursts. But I don't think it's that kind of storm that is threatening to-day. Alam thinks that more likely it will be a sandstorm, and that won't be so pleasant."

Travelling was difficult that day, for they found themselves in what had evidently been a region at one time rent by earthquakes. The ground was seamed with great fissures, some of them narrow and shallow, others deep and gaping.

The drivers of the cars had to exercise the greatest care and make so many semicircles and detours that Brick declared that before long they would meet themselves coming back.

The captain and Don were fortunate enough to escape the traps that nature had laid for them, but the professor was not so lucky. Shortly before the hour when they had planned to stop and pitch camp, there came a loud crash in the rear and a frenzied tooting of a horn.

"His car's gone into one of the cracks!" exclaimed Don, as he shut off the power and applied the brakes.

The captain also halted abruptly, and the inmates of the first two cars rushed back to help their comrades. They found the professor and Abdullah making frantic efforts to jack up their car, one side of which lay at an acute angle in one of the cracks.

"Either of you hurt?" asked the captain, as he hurried up to them.

"No," answered the professor. "But I don't know how badly the car may be damaged. It sounded as though something smashed when it lurched in."

"It's the water tank!" shouted Don, in dismay, as he saw a stream pouring out over one side.

They hurried about and got all the receptacles

they could find, but were able to save only a slight quantity of the precious fluid.

The loss would have been serious at any time, but was doubly so now, as the supplies in the other cars had already been exhausted and practically all their surplus had been in the third car.

"Bad business," muttered the captain, his brow furrowed with anxiety.

They worked like beavers, and finally, by their united efforts, got the car out on level ground. Luckily, it was not badly damaged, sufficiently so, however, to detain them a considerable time while they made the necessary repairs.

And now for the first time the Americans learned what thirst in the desert really meant. What water was left in the container was barely sufficient to moisten their parched lips. They dared not drink it all and the very knowledge that they could not made their thirst more acute.

Everything depended on their getting quickly to the next water hole, about eighty miles away. If their cars should break down! They did not dare think of the fate that would await them then.

As soon as their repairs were completed they went on—on under that terrible, scorching sun. They did not dare stop, even in the hottest hours of the day. Their throats were parched, their tongues swollen. Water! Water! How they longed for it, as they kept on grimly, spurred by their terrible need and torturing apprehension.

Fifty—sixty—seventy miles were covered. Now they were nearing their goal. Hope began to revive. Five, six, seven more—and then, while Don was feverishly peering ahead for the coveted oasis, Brick touched his arm.

"Look at that yellow cloud out there," he said, pointing towards the distant horizon.

Don looked and was appalled.

"See how it's coming whirling towards us!" he exclaimed. "That means business. It looks like pictures I've seen of the beginning of a Kansas cyclone."

A loud blast from the car in front showed that its occupants also were alive to the menace concealed in that twisting, lowering cloud. The captain slowed up, and in a moment the other cars stopped close behind him.

"Alam says that a sandstorm is coming," explained the captain hurriedly. "We've got to hurry and park these cars together as a bulwark against it. Then we'll lie down on the lee side of them with blankets over our faces to keep out the sand and wait for the storm to blow over."

Under the direction of Alam and Abdullah, the cars were arranged in a line, their sides in the direction from which the storm was approaching. It was coming now with terrible rapidity.

None of the party was ignorant of the danger. More than once entire caravans had been covered by mounds of sand and had left only their bleached bones to tell of the tragedy.

First came an exceedingly hot wind, that made everyone feel, as all lay at full length in the shelter of the cars, as though a blast had come from the open door of a red-hot furnace. This carried with it innumerable particles of flying sand, scouts, as it

vere, coming before the real storm, as though to
earch out and mark the weak points of the prey to
e attacked. The sand penetrated everywhere,
inding every crevice, working its way even through
he texture of the blankets like the points of so
nany needles. It was irritating, torturing in the
xtreme. But it was only a preliminary. The real
torm was yet to come.

Then, suddenly, it was upon them, coming with
a roar like thunder, blinding, smothering, over-
whelming! It seemed as though a giant hand had
reached into the sand of the desert and flung the
handfuls in tons down on the tortured travellers.

All cowered in their blankets before the storm's
ury, so unlike what any of them except Alam and
Abdullah had ever known before.

"Sounds like the howl of a wild beast, doesn't
t?" asked Don of Brick.

He had to shout at the top of his voice to make
himself heard, but he did not mind this in his
nstinct for companionship.

"Sure does," Brick shouted back. "But we can
tand its howling if it doesn't sink its teeth into us."

There was a sound like that of ripping canvas.

"There go the curtains of the car," surmised
Brick dolefully. Then both boys fell silent, and
ach wrapped himself more closely in his own
blanket.

For a brief time after this the cars acted as a
bulwark against the worst fury of the storm. But
only for a time. Before long the sand had heaped
up against their sides in drifts many feet high. The
ars themselves were invaded. The sand covered

the wheels, the sides, and finally the tops of the machines. Then it reached over the tops and began to search out the crouching travellers, for all the world like a monster groping about with hot fingers for its victims.

They, in the meantime, were suffering intensely not only with apprehension of their possible fate but from keen physical pain.

For a period that seemed endless the torture continued. Don's eyes were smarting with the sand that forced itself between his closed lids. His lips were cracked. His mouth was sore and his nose was bleeding. He felt as though he were smothering. The mound of sand that had formed above him seemed to be pressing the breath out of him. He had never endured such suffering.

He moved backward a little in the hope of dislodging some of the intolerable weight. As he did so, the ground beneath him suddenly gave way and he felt himself falling.

He made a desperate effort to save himself, but his hands were so tightly enfolded in the blanket that he could grasp nothing. Down he went falling, falling!

CHAPTER XIII

JUST IN TIME

Don's body, in its mummy-like swathings of blankets, ceased its descent with a sudden shock that jarred him from head to heels.

It was several moments before his head cleared and he could realise what had happened. Then he remembered the gaping cracks in the earth, some of them several feet wide, that seamed the surface of the ground over which they had been travelling.

When he had lain down in his blanket, he must have failed to notice, in the hurry and confusion, that he was near the edge of one of these yawning holes. In his attempt to find relief from the load of sand above him, he had slipped over the edge.

Luckily he had gone down feet foremost. Had he fallen headfirst, death would have been inevitable.

But the little feeling of exultation that came to him from this circumstance quickly vanished. For though death had been deferred, it seemed only for a brief time. The weight of his body had wedged his feet tightly in the narrowing sides of the hole, and he felt as though they were clamped in an iron vice.

He could see nothing. He had succeeded in wrenching his head from the close folds of the blanket, and, opening his smarting eyes, he tried to look about him. But he was forced quickly to wrap the blanket around his head again to shelter it from the sand that was coming down into the cavity in a cloud.

His heart sank as he realised how fast the cavity was filling. Soon the sand was up to his knees and was rapidly climbing higher. He was trapped! He was being buried alive!

He was too young to die. Everything in him clamoured for life. The blood ran strongly through his veins. He was only standing on the threshold of life, life that had stretched out before him with all its dreams, its hopes, its wonderful possibilities —the life of which he seemed about to be deprived.

Now the sand had reached his waist!

The sand reached his throat!

His lungs, compressed by the weight of sand, seemed to be bursting. His breath came in long, laboured gasps. Sparks of fire danced before his eyes. He prayed. He felt his senses going.

What was that? A shout? His name?

"Don! Don!" came in anguished tones from above, echoed by other cries.

By a tremendous effort he steadied his swimming brain. Something touched him, groped for him.

Before the sand had reached his waist, he had freed his arms from the blanket and held them above his head. Now he reached out his hands and grasped a pole. It had a knob at the end that offered a hold, and he gripped it as a drowning man grips a rope thrown to him.

"Hold tight!" came the stentorian voice of the captain. "Keep your head, my boy. We'll get you out."

Eager hands at the other end of the pole pulled strongly and steadily, and Don held on with the clutch of desperation, though he felt as though his arms were being wrenched from their sockets. Little by little, but surely, he felt himself being drawn up. At last he was within reach of his rescuers. Then two powerful arms came down and caught his, and he was pulled out and laid on the solid earth.

That was all he remembered for the next half-hour. Then he came to consciousness to find himself being rubbed and chafed by his uncles, whose eyes were wet with tears of which they were not ashamed, while Brick stood by, frankly weeping, and even the impassive Arabs showing signs of being deeply moved.

Don tried to speak, but his voice sounded strangely far away and incoherent, and his Uncle Frank stopped him.

"Not now, my dear boy," he said gently. "Plenty of time for talk later. The only thing that matters now is that you are alive. Just lie still for a time, and when you are a little stronger you can tell us all about it."

Don was so exhausted that he needed little urging. He lay quietly for a few moments, noting little except that the storm had passed and rejoicing that he was still in the land of the living. Then he dropped off into a heavy sleep, from which he woke many hours later, quite restored to his usual self.

It was then that he heard the full story of the happenings following his disappearance.

Some little time after he had fallen, the worst

fury of the storm had abated, and Brick, who had been lying near him, reached out his arm and to his surprise met only vacancy where Don had been. Even then he was only slightly startled, for he thought that Don must have shifted to some spot a little way off to get in a more comfortable position. But when he had called to him and received no answer he had become genuinely alarmed, and had shouted until the captain and the professor came hurrying to him.

A frantic search had ensued, a search which had ended in the discovery of the deep crevasse near the spot where Don and Teddy had lain. The inference to be drawn was obvious, and Don's uncles had fought their way to the cars and unearthed one of the tent poles with which they had rushed to the hole, their hearts torn with apprehension lest they were too late.

"It was a mighty close call, sure enough," said Don. "I had about given myself up for lost. Another minute and I wouldn't have had sense enough to grab the pole."

"Even then we would have got you," said the captain, with grim determination. "We would have formed a human chain and one of us would have been let down headfirst to pull you out. Thank God that you are alive and safe!"

While Don had been sleeping, Alam and Abdullah had gone with vessels to the well that they had so nearly reached before the storm had come upon them, and had returned with a supply of water to last over night.

The experience had a sobering effect upon them

all. It showed them by what a frail tenure life was held in the desert. It brought home to them, as never before, the risks they had set out to encounter. At no time until they should return to civilisation would there be anything but a step between them and death.

There was no thought of going any farther that night. They were all in too sore and smarting a condition after the battle with the storm to think of doing anything else but rest. In addition, the cars were so covered with sand that it would take hours to release them and get them in shape for the continuation of the journey.

How bad that condition was they did not realise until the next day dawned. It took hours of hard work before the cars were freed. And that was not all, for all articles and packages in them were so permeated with sand that they had to be gone over with care. Sand had also got into the bearings of the machinery to such an extent that the engines had to be taken apart and rubbed smooth and thoroughly oiled if serious damage was to be averted.

So, instead of one, it was two full days that were required before they were in shape to start. The captain chafed at the delay, for every day they lost diminished by so much their supplies for the journey, which had been very carefully calculated.

Teddy, too, worried over the delay, for fear of what might be happening to his father. A day lost might mean the difference between life and death.

Don's special cause of worry he kept to himself. It concerned itself with the matter of the emeralds.

He had never been free from uneasiness since the unlucky day when that secret had slipped out, perhaps to be overheard by rascals who would seek to profit by it.

As long as they could keep going on their intended schedule, there was no danger of their being overtaken. But many more such delays might mean being overhauled by a robber gang, if a plan of robbery were in the wind.

So he worked like a Trojan at the machinery, together with his uncles, and breathed a sigh of immense relief when at last the task was finished.

He had said to himself that they would make unusual speed on their next lap in order to atone for the delay. But to his disappointment he found that the going was much more difficult than it had been up to this time.

The hard, good road gave place to soft and shifting sand, as they advanced towards Fort Hassi Inifel. In the vicinity of this oasis there were great sand dunes or hillocks, rising in some cases to a height of two or three hundred feet. Some of these they had to surmount, with a strain on their engines and a lessening of speed. Others they had to go around, sometimes travelling two miles to make one as the crow flies.

Then, too, it became increasingly difficult to be sure they were on the right track. The great storm of a few days before had so changed the form and character of these dunes that old landmarks had in some cases been obliterated, and Alam often had to halt the expedition while he made sure of the right path to follow. When he finally made up his mind, his judgment always proved right, but the net result was that they were "making haste slowly."

At Hassi Inifel, which had formerly been a French military station, they found an old block house with two comfortable rooms, where they got a good night's rest and also enjoyed the luxury of a bath.

They did not tarry there, however, and the next day were off at dawn. Now, again, the country began to change. From an expanse of sandy plains, with their bluish and gilded dunes, they came into a desolate and gloomy region, strewn with sharp rocks and abounding in deep ravines.

They were in the Tademait Plateau, the black rock region, so called from the peculiar stones that covered the road and that looked as though they had received a coat of black varnish.

There was a certain relief in getting away from the flat surface and finding themselves in a hilly country. But at the same time it required much more vigilance in driving. The way in places was precipitous, with deep chasms on both sides. And, looking over the edges of those chasms, they could see the bones of camels that had lost their footing and fallen to sure death below. The sight was one calculated to insure great care in driving, and there was very little conversation going on when the cars were skirting one of those perilous places, as the driver had to keep his eyes glued on the path ahead of him.

It was hard work going up some of these steep ascents, but it was still harder going down, and much more dangerous. Even when the power was shut off and the brakes applied, the mere momentum of the cars on some of the steep grades carried them along at a pace far too rapid for the peace of mind of the travellers. Often, too, the path was strewn with boulders, and only the most skilful manœuvring could avoid them.

It was on the second day out from Hassi Inifel that the car which Don was driving reached the top of an especially precipitous descent. The captain's car had already started down the slope and was merely creeping along about three hundred feet ahead.

Don started down, shutting off his power and applying the brakes. To his consternation, the car commenced to gather speed. He pressed again upon the brake, but the car kept going still faster. On and on it went, coasting down the hill by sheer force of gravity.

Don looked at Brick, his face as white as chalk.

"The brakes don't work!" he gasped, in dire dismay.

CHAPTER XIV

CLOSE TO DEATH

"WHAT?" cried Teddy, in alarm.

"They don't work—the brakes," repeated Don. "They're out of order. You'd better jump, Brick. It's your best chance."

"Are you going to jump too?" asked Teddy.

"No," replied Don. "I've got to stick to the wheel, or we'll smash into Uncle Frank's car. But you jump, and jump quick. You can make it."

"I won't do it," declared Teddy stoutly. "We'll stick it out together.

There was no time for argument. Don blew a series of blasts from his horn as a warning to the car ahead, which they were now approaching at a tremendous rate of speed.

He saw his Uncle Frank poke out his head and look back. It was evident that Captain Sturdy grasped the situation at once, for his own car swerved instantly to the left of the narrow road until it was on the very edge of a deep chasm.

There it came to a stop, leaving all the space that was possible between it and the great cliff that loomed up on the other side of the road.

"Could he make it?" Don asked himself, as he studied the narrow passage between the first car and the cliff. It looked frightfully small. If he failed, if it were not wide enough, the two cars would crash and both be hurled into the abyss. And that meant certain death for all concerned.

The car was whizzing along now at a terrific speed. Don must utilise every inch of that narrow space, for it was evidently only a matter of inches.

On they went, with the boy's hand clutching the wheel with a grasp of iron. There must be no wavering! He must make it!

Don did not see the agonised face of his uncle watching him in awful apprehension. He felt Brick's grip tighten on the seat, but he paid no attention to it. He must make that passage!

There was a rush, a roar, a moment when Don's heart stood still, and then he had passed the other car by a margin of a fraction of an inch and was making at railroad speed towards the bottom of the incline.

If there had been a curve in the road, he and Teddy would have been doomed. The car would have been going too fast to make the turn.

But the Providence that watches over the brave was with Don. The road broadened out into a wide plateau. As soon as it reached the level, the car began to slacken speed, and gradually came to a stop of its own accord.

Brick jumped out and Don followed. The reaction was on him now, and his knees trembled so that he could scarcely stand. But it was a smiling face, if a pale one, with which he greeted his uncles, as they brought their cars to a stop and rushed up to throw their arms around him.

"Going to scold me for reckless driving?" he managed to joke.

"Reckless!" exclaimed his Uncle Frank, who was as much agitated as the boy himself. "It was the finest exhibition of nerve and skill I've ever seen. Not one in a hundred could have negotiated that narrow passage without going smash against the cliff or knocking my car over into the chasm. It was a situation that might have tested the nerve of a veteran driver, let alone a boy of fourteen. My heart was in my mouth while I watched you come dashing down the hill."

"As far as nerve is concerned, Teddy had just as much as I had," declared Don generously. "He had a chance to jump and refused it to stick with me. And where another fellow might have rattled me by howling and jumping around, he just gritted his teeth and didn't say a word."

"Good for Teddy!" commended the captain. "You two make a fine pair."

"It wasn't that I wasn't scared though," said Teddy, with a grin. "According to the stories you read, this red mop of mine ought to have turned as white as snow."

"Well, all's well that ends well," said the professor thankfully. "And now we'll have to camp here for a while and see what was the matter with the brakes. Full of sand, no doubt, that prevented their working properly. And while we're about it, we might as well overhaul the other cars as well."

Despite their eagerness to get on, all felt the good sense of the suggestion, and they decided to call it a day as far as travelling was concerned.

This time their work was done under better conditions than any they had known up till now.

There were rocks and cliffs that afforded shade. And this was the more grateful to them because by this time all the party were suffering to a greater or less extent from sunburn and blisters. One cannot battle with the heat of the Sahara without paying the penalty.

The repairs to the brakes and other parts of the machinery that proved to need attention took a good deal longer than Don's uncles had anticipated, despite the fact that all worked like beavers, except, of course, Alam and Abdullah who had not the slightest knowledge of machinery and who would have hindered rather than helped.

Teddy, though not very familiar with cars, had a natural aptitude for mechanics and was of considerable help to Don. The skill and cleverness of the latter were a source of unfailing admiration to his friend.

"If you ever go broke, you can get a good job in a garage," Brick said. "You must have had a good deal of experience back home."

"Yes," replied Don. "Our chauffeur was a dandy, and he was always ready to teach me what he knew."

"What kind of place did you have?" asked Brick.

"It's a good big house and there are plenty of trees around it," replied Don. "We have a house-keeper, Mrs. Roscoe, and her husband acts as a handy man about the place. Then we had a maid, Jennie Jenks, who was always chewing gum. I'm willing to bet that if I could see her right now she'd have a wad of gum in her mouth. I wish I were on the old place this minute. Though, after all," he added mournfully, "I haven't taken much comfort in it for the last two years. I got so restless I couldn't stand it. That's one reason my uncles were willing to bring me along with them, so as to get my mind off my troubles. What's the use of a home, after all," he added, with sudden bitterness, "if there's no father or mother or sister in it?"

"I know," said Brick sympathetically. "It's tough on a fellow. But I hope the time will come when they will be in it. There's a chance, anyhow."

"Yes," replied Don sadly, "there is a chance as long as I don't know actually that they are dead. But that chance grows slimmer with every month that passes without news of them. But, no matter how foolish it may seem, I have a feeling that they're still alive. I couldn't give you any reason for the feeling, but I have it just the same. And just as soon as I'm old enough, I'm going to spend my life hunting for them. Ruth's a dandy girl, and we were great chums. I miss her a lot."

"I wish I could help you look for them," said Brick earnestly. "That would pay some of the debt I owe you for coming into this desert to try to find my father."

"Try to find him?" repeated Don. "We're going to find him! And we're going to find the Cave of Emeralds too. I never felt surer of that than I do this minute."

The necessary work on the cars took all that day and so far into the next morning that it was not practicable to start until the late afternoon. It was a relief to have a little leisure time on their hands, and Don and Brick employed it by strolling up the slope, down which their runaway car had coasted. They took with them Professor Bruce's field glasses.

From the top of the hill they had an extensive view of the plain beyond.

"Big cloud of dust over there," remarked Brick. "Perhaps there's another sandstorm coming up."

"Hope not," replied Don. "The one we've already had is enough for a lifetime. No, it isn't that," he added, as he scrutinised the dust cloud more closely. "I can see moving figures. It must be a caravan. And it seems to be making pretty rapid time, too," he went on, looking through the glasses.

"Rather unusual for them to be travelling so fast in the hottest part of the day," remarked Brick.

Their pulses quickened as the same thought struck them, and they strained their eyes as the caravan approached. Don took another long look through the glasses.

"I know one of those men!" he exclaimed. "That one riding in front! He's the man with the scar!"

CHAPTER XV

TROUBLE BREWING

DON and Brick looked at each other with consternation in their eyes and a sinking in their hearts.

"So those fellows did overhear us that day when

we were talking about the emeralds in Tuggurt!" exclaimed Brick. "Let me have those glasses a moment, Don!" and he, too, looked through the field glasses.

"I'm afraid they did hear us—and understand," replied Don. "That was a most unlucky day for us."

"Of course," said Brick, clutching at a little shred of hope, "they may be on other business in the desert, and not have us in mind at all."

"Not a chance," replied Don. "If that were so, you'd see some packs on their camels. But if you'll notice, there are just as many camels as there are riders. They're travelling light."

"There's a pretty big crowd of them, too," said Brick thoughtfully.

The boys counted the Arabs as well as they could, and made out that there were fully eighteen in the party. All of them had rifles, and it looked much more like a military expedition than an ordinary peaceful caravan.

"We must get back to camp as soon as possible and tell my uncles about it," said Don, suiting the action to the word and hurrying down the trail, with Brick close at his heels.

Captain Sturdy was standing near one of the cars as the boys came up almost out of breath, and one glance at their faces was enough to tell him that something out of the ordinary had happened.

"What is it?" he asked quietly.

They told him of what they had seen, and the captain listened attentively.

"Eighteen, you say?" he queried.

"We counted that many," replied Don. "But in the dust we might have missed one or two. There are fully eighteen."

"That's three to one," mused the captain. "Pretty heavy odds. Get your rifles ready. How far off were they?"

"Not more than a mile when we came away," replied Don, "and they were travelling fast."

"They may be here at any minute, then," said the captain. "Ah, there's one of them now!" he exclaimed, as a camel and his rider came into view at the top of the ridge.

Had the cars been ready to start, the captain would probably have considered it wiser to avoid trouble and resume the journey instantly. They could easily have outdistanced the newcomers, and perhaps have seen them no more. But the supplies had been unpacked while the repairs were going on, and half an hour at least would have been needed to get them in their places.

That the sight of the little encampment had been an unexpected one to the caravan was evident from the suddenness with which the foremost rider pulled his mount to a stop at the top of the hill. He came no farther until he had been joined by the rest of his companions. Then an excited parley ensued, at the end of which the party came slowly down the slope.

They halted at a distance of about two hundred yards, and then their leader rode slowly forward, after dropping his weapon to the ground and extending his empty palms to indicate that his intentions were peaceful.

"Go meet him, Alam, and find out all you can about him and what he wants," directed the captain. "If he shows the least sign of treachery, we'll fill him full of lead."

Alam went to meet the leader, and an animated conversation ensued. At the end of a few minutes, Alam came back and reported.

The man had told him that the caravan was on its way to Insalah. The date harvest was at hand, and his party expected to go back, laden with fruit, to Tuggurt. That explained why they were carrying no merchandise with them now. They had been surprised at coming upon the captain's party. They had no idea that a car expedition was in the desert. They had nothing but goodwill in their hearts, and were pained at the suspicious attitude of the foreigners. They would willingly stop and make camp with them, and then go on, for a little way at least together.

"Humph!" sniffed the captain unbelievingly. "That's what he says. What do you think of it, Alam?"

"The man is a dog," replied Alam. "His heart is black and his tongue is full of lies."

"He told a falsehood when he said that he did not know of the expedition," broke in Don, "for I saw him in the crowd when the cars pulled out of Tuggurt."

"He is a bad man," resumed Alam. "He rests under the frown of Allah. I knew him in Tuggurt. He has been in jail many times. A caravan carries goods both ways. These are riding camels, not pack camels, that he has with him. His men are scum, robbers. He has followed you, travelling day and night. He means evil."

"He is one of the men who tried to rob me the night I first met you," said Brick. "I know him by his scar."

"I guess that's enough," said the captain. "It only confirms what I suspected from the first. Go back to him, Alam, and tell him this:

"The Feringhee is glad to know that you cherish no evil intentions. This is well, for he has machine-guns in his cars that could wipe out your whole company, if you meant him ill. He does not think that it would be well to make camp together, for the plateau is small. He urges, then, that you go forward while he stays, or, if you wish, he will go forward while you stay. Peace be with you."

"I guess that will give them food for thought," the captain remarked, as Alam went forward to deliver the message.

They saw a malignant scowl settle on the leader's face as Alam talked to him. His lips were drawn back from his teeth in the same ferocious snarl that Don had seen on the night he had rescued Teddy. It was perhaps lucky for Alam that the man had dropped his gun before he rode out for the parley. He turned abruptly and rode back to his companions, and Alam returned to the group awaiting him.

"What did he say?" asked the captain.

"That he and his party would go on," replied Alam. "That since the Feringhee did not wish his company, he would not force it upon him."

The Americans and their two helpers stood alert

and ready for any emergency as, after excited gesticulations, the newcomers filed past at a little distance, the leader casting a farewell glance at Don's party that was like the glint in the eyes of a rattlesnake.

The relief they felt at getting rid of the unwelcome caravan was only momentary, for all felt that they had only deferred the problem instead of settling it. That evil gang was still to be reckoned with. No one believed for a moment that the Arabs had given up their purpose.

"They must have done some tall travelling to catch up with us," mused the captain.

"They've probably done about eighteen hours a day," replied the professor. "Even then they'd never have done it, if it hadn't been for the delays we've experienced. As a matter of fact, they were surprised themselves when they came upon us so suddenly.

"What do you suppose they will do now, Alam?" asked the captain.

"They will camp when night comes and lie in wait for us," predicted Alam.

"Not an extremely pleasant prospect," remarked the captain. "We'd be in separate cars, and it would be easy enough for them to surround and cut off one of the cars. Then by threatening to kill the captives they could try to bring the rest of us to terms."

"If they are after the emeralds we're supposed to be hunting for, I should think it would be wiser on their part to wait until we'd found them and then ambush us on our return," remarked the professor, in some perplexity.

"That may have been their original plan," returned the captain. "They may have meant simply to have kept within striking distance and attack us at the proper time. But now they've caught up with us, their purpose may be served just as well by capturing us now if possible and making us lead them in the search for the emeralds. After that our usefulness would be finished, and then— well, you can guess the rest."

The others guessed very readily, and their guess was not a pleasant one.

"Let not the masters be troubled," put in Alam placidly. "The dogs will wait in vain."

"What do you mean?" asked the captain quickly.

"They will wait in vain, praise be to Allah," Alam repeated. "Your servant knows another pass through these rocks that is known to few. The way is rough and long and roundabout, but when we come from it we will be far in advance of these robbers."

"Good!" roared the captain delightedly. "Alam you're a brick! You may not know what that means, but you're it. We made no mistake in bringing you along. Let's pack and start."

CHAPTER XVI

THE TRAIL GROWS WARM

THERE was no need for urging haste in the packing for all were eager to get away from the proximity of the men who constituted the greatest peril the party in search of Mr. Allison and the Cave of Emeralds had yet met in the desert.

In less time than Don had believed possible, the party was ready to start. The route that Alam had in mind made it necessary for them to go back for a distance of about three miles over the path they had traversed. There they turned sharply to the left and took up their journey over a rough forbidding road that fully justified Alam's description of it.

But the Americans were in no mood to be critical, and they kept along, though at a greatly diminished rate of speed, owing to the boulders that strewed the district and required the utmost skill in driving to avoid.

Darkness came, and camp was made for the night, the captain and the professor relinquished the idea they had first entertained of travelling at night in that perilous region, for the way was hard enough to traverse in the full light of day.

The first streak of dawn, however, found the travellers on their way, and now they found that the worst part of the route lay behind them. The way broadened out into a sandy plain where the ground was hard, and they bowled along at a rapid rate.

Their compass told them that they had described a wide semi-circle that had certainly put them far to the front of the robbers' caravan.

"Now let them follow," laughed the captain, at their first stop for a meal. "A stern chase is a long chase."

"Still, we want to remember that we are not yet out of the woods," said the professor, with a smile. "If I can use that expression in this desert waste. Those fellows are not going to give up the chase so easily."

"And if they don't catch us going, they'll lay for us coming back," put in Don.

"Oh, it's quite possible that we haven't seen the last of them," agreed the captain.

"Gazo el Beno will keep to the trail," warned Alam. "His heart is hot with the hope of gain."

"So that's the leader's name, is it?" said Don. "Well, Gazo el Beno would better give this party a wide berth unless he wants his bones to rest with those of his fathers."

"I'm getting pretty well fed up with him and his gang myself, and the next time we meet, my finger may be a little careless with the trigger," added Captain Sturdy.

"Look!" exclaimed Don suddenly. "What is that over there? It looks like a big lake."

"Impossible!" declared the captain, as he followed the direction of Don's pointing finger. "There's no lake within hundreds of miles."

Yet his scepticism was shaken for a moment, for far off, near the horizon, was what seemed to be a large body of water, the movement of the waves being plainly discernible.

"Seeing is believing," he muttered, as he rubbed his eyes and looked again.

Professor Bruce, who had been observing the phenomenon, shook his head.

"No such luck," he said, with a smile. "What you're looking at is a mirage. They're often seen in the Sahara."

"Then it isn't water, after all!" cried Brick, in great disappointment. "It's just old Nature fooling us."

"Something like that," agreed the professor. "It's a mere optical illusion, due to the varying density of the strata of air. The air is hottest near the sand; the rays coming down from the sky are bent upwards; the eye receives an impression resembling that produced by the reflection of sky light from water. And what renders the illusion more perfect is the flickering, due to the air currents, which causes an appearance like a breeze playing over water."

"I see," said Brick, who, however, did not see quite clearly, but was willing to let it go at that.

"I confess that for a moment it had me guessing," admitted the captain. "But now that our hopes of getting a bath are dashed, suppose we get going once more."

The illusion persisted for hours, and it grew so tantalising that after a while they turned their eyes away from it and fixed their attention wholly on the road.

Fortune favoured them, and they made good time for the next two days, the cars behaving perfectly.

At Insalah they found one of the largest oases they had seen since the start of their trip. And here for the first time, except for the little trickling springs, they had the refreshing sight of flowing water. There were hundreds of wells, and the water from these was conducted through troughs and ditches to the foot of the many palm trees, thus furnishing irrigation for the dates that were grown there in great profusion.

They found here also one of the gasoline stations that the French had established in the desert, and were able to fill their tanks to the limit and also replenish their stores of water. They made the most of their opportunities, for it was the last place of any importance that they would meet before reaching the Hoggar Plateau.

The French officers, here as everywhere, were most hospitable, and urged the Americans to prolong their stay. But they had to decline, for to their other reasons for haste was added that of Gazo el Beno and his gang of rascals plodding along somewhere behind them in the desert.

The country was now changing. The flat expanse of the desert was being replaced by rocky elevations that grew ever higher and higher as they proceeded. The nights grew colder, and often, after a day of sweltering heat, they were glad enough to seek the protection of the despised blankets that had seemed so needless a part of their equipment.

Vegetation, too, became more abundant. Clumps of sagebrush and cactus made the desert resemble some parts of Arizona. And with these evidences of plant life, however dwarfed and stunted, came traces of game. Jackals disturbed the camp at night with their howling, silenced in more cases than one by a shot from Don's rifle.

They caught sight at times also of gazelles and foxes, whose skins the captain was very anxious to obtain for his collection. Several times, when the party was resting in the heat of the day, the captain and Don would sally forth for an hour or two and come back with spoils.

On these occasions they always consulted Alam, for the Arab had what he regarded as an infallible method of foretelling whether the shooting would be good or bad.

"What are the signs, Alam?" Don would inquire.

The Arab would take from his pocket two kola nuts, one end of which was more pointed than another. These he would throw in the air. If they fell with both pointed ends towards the thrower, the signs were good. If both sharp ends were pointing the other way, the outlook was bad. If one point was towards him and the other away from him, the process had to be repeated. And the odd thing about it was that the signs were apparently justified. A mere coincidence, according to the Americans, but one that brought profound satisfaction to Alam.

Don's shooting on these trips delighted his uncle.

The new rifle worked like a charm. Up to that time, most of Don's markmanship had been developed at stationary targets. Now he had an opportunity of perfecting himself in shooting at moving objects, and more than once he brought down his quarry with a shot that the captain himself could scarcely have bettered.

"Good work, my boy," congratulated his uncle, on one occasion when Don brought down a jackal that had almost got out of range. "That kind of shooting is going to come in mighty handy, if the Tuaregs try any of their funny business on us."

The third day out from Insalah, Alam pointed to a thin blue line on the horizon.

"The Hoggar Mountains," he announced.

A thrill went through the members of the party. Now they were close upon the objects of their expedition. Somewhere in this vicinity, if anywhere, they might hope to find the man of whom they were in search, if he were still alive. Somewhere on this great plateau or in the depths of the mountain ranges might lie the Cave of Emeralds. Somewhere in the same district they might have the luck of coming upon the City of Brass. And of special interest to the professor, was the chance of finding the mysterious Cemetery of the Elephants.

Now especial care was necessary, for the plateau was the dwelling place of the Tuaregs, the fierce desert folk that lived on plunder. And the searchers must contemplate the probability that before long they would have to abandon their cars and proceed on foot. This would greatly increase the dangers to which they would be exposed, for in case of attack the cars were so many small forts that afforded no mean protection. And when all was said and done, the fact remained that there were only six in the party.

But their hearts were stout and their weapons good, and although they realised their danger more clearly than they had before, there was no faint-heartedness or wavering. They had put their hands to the plough and would not turn back.

The party now proceeded with great caution, keeping the cars much closer together than they had been in the habit of doing. The use of the horn was abandoned, lest the sound should reach hostile ears, and their eyes ranged the landscape, intent upon discovering the first sign of danger.

Brick, especially, was on the alert. He was travelling in the vicinity of the place he had been when the caravan with which he was journeying had been raided. Suddenly he gave vent to an exclamation and clutched Don's arm.

"This is the place we were camping when the Tuaregs came down upon us!" he cried, pointing to a small plateau. "And there, on the side of the hill, is the rock behind which Alam and I were hiding."

CHAPTER XVII

A NIGHT OF TERROR

"ARE you sure?" asked Don, as he slackened speed.

"Dead sure," was the answer. "What happened that night was burned into my memory so that I can't forget it."

At that moment, the car in front stopped, and the captain and Alam climbed out.

"Alam tells me that this is where the raid on Mr. Allison's caravan took place," said Captain Sturdy.

"Just what Brick was telling me this very minute!" exclaimed Don.

"If both agree, they must be right," remarked the captain. "We're in the enemy's country now, and what happened to Teddy's party may happen to us. But I'm glad that the trail is getting warm. In what direction did the raiders go after the fight was over?" he went on, turning to Alam.

The latter pointed in a direction a little south of west. It was a precipitous region with peaks rising high towards the skies, one of them being fully eight thousand feet above the level of the sea.

"Doesn't look much like a place for cars," was Don's comment

"We'll go as far as we can, and then, for the rest, we'll have to be guided by circumstances," replied Captain Sturdy.

They resumed their journey, changing their direction so as to conform to the information given by Alam. The going was slow and arduous, and in places their path was bordered by precipices that made the boys shudder as they cast glances into the yawning depths beneath.

Teddy was in a fever of excitement, now that he felt he was approaching the fastnesses where his father might be held in captivity. Torturing doubts beset him at times as to whether his father might not long since have passed from the land of the living. But he dismissed these, as far as he was able, and clung desperately to hope. And in this he was seconded by Don.

"You're better off than I am," affirmed Don, with deep sadness in his tone. "There's a good chance that you'll find your father alive and soon, while as for me——"

His voice choked, and he turned away to conceal his emotion. Was his life to be forever shadowed by the grief of separation from those who were dearer to him than life?

The day was sweltering, one of the hottest they had yet encountered in the desert. The sun beat down with terrific force. The breaths they drew in seemed as if they would scorch their lungs. They were drenched through and through with perspiration, and their clothes clung to them almost as closely as though part of their bodies.

Because of this, they welcomed the coming of the night as they had never done before when at last a halt was called on a shelving rock platform in a mountain pass. On one side was a high cliff, and on the other side of the path, which was about twenty feet wide, was a deep ravine.

They would have preferred a wider space for their encampment, and for the last hour had been looking for one as they went along. But nothing better offered, and they chose the best at hand.

Alam usually went to sleep as soon as the evening meal was finished, but that night he seemed unusually restless. He had frequent conferences with Abdullah, who seemed to share his uneasiness.

"What's the matter, Alam?" asked Don, who for some time had been observing him curiously.

"Your uncle's servant thinks a storm is coming," was the reply. "He feels it in the air."

"Well, if that's so, I'm glad we're up so high in the hills," replied the boy. "A sandstorm can't bother us badly up here."

"It is not a sandstorm that is coming," explained Alam. "It is rain."

There was an instant commotion among the members of the party.

"Glory hallelujah!" cried Don. "Rain in this desert! I almost forgot there was such a word. I'll be more glad to see that storm than I ever was before in my life."

"It can't come too soon for me," said Brick. "I'd like to sit out in it all night. It'll be the finest kind of a shower bath."

The captain and the professor, though less exuberant in their demonstrations, seemed to welcome the prospect with as much satisfaction as the boys. But the Arabs showed no trace of exultation.

"What's the matter with you two?" Don demanded. "I should think you'd be delighted, and you look as glum as though you were going to a funeral."

"Yes, what is it, Alam?" asked Professor Bruce.

"Has the master ever seen a rainstorm in the desert?" Alam asked respectfully.

"No, but I'm glad I'm going to," was the answer. "I suppose it is much like a rainstorm anywhere else."

"The desert is terrible in everything it does," was the rather cryptic remark of the Arab.

"I notice it doesn't do anything by halves," put in Teddy. "Sandstorms, for instance."

"What are you trying to get at, Alam? Do you think there is any danger?" asked Don.

"Not if we were out on the sand plains," said Alam. "But up in these mountains there is danger. The wind will come with the rain, and its force is greater than the might of man. The rain will come down like the ocean. It will be as though the sky had broken."

By this time the jubilation of the Americans had departed. They knew that when Alam spoke he spoke soberly. He was no breeder of panic.

"What do you think we had better do?" asked the captain anxiously. "Perhaps we had better spend the night in the shelter of the cars."

"No," replied Alam. "Not in the cars. There will be more danger there than anywhere else. They may be washed away. We must secure them as well as we can, and we ourselves must seek refuge in the rocks."

A thrill of alarm ran through the party. If the cars were lost, they themselves were doomed. To be left stranded in this desert meant almost certain death. They could not carry enough water and supplies to meet their needs. Never before had they realised how closely their own safety was bound up with that of the cars.

For a moment all sat as though stunned, and then at the sharp and quick direction of the captain, they sprang to action. The cars were drawn as close to the side of the cliff as possible. Then the heaviest boulders to be found were rolled on the farther side of the cars, so as to keep them from being blown towards the precipice beyond. In addition, the ropes that had been brought along to draw water from the wells were wound around and around the cars, and the ends tied to what projecting spurs of the cliff could be found.

It seemed, when all was finished, that no power of the elements, however tremendous, could tear the cars from their fastenings. But the Americans would have felt better if they could have seen that Alam and Abdullah shared their confidence.

"Don't you think that will hold them all right, Alam?" asked Don, as he finished tying the last knot.

"We are in the hands of Allah," was the non-committal reply.

The wind was rising rapidly, and it swept down the gorge with a howl like that of a wild beast.

"To the rocks!" directed Alam. "We must hasten! The time is short!"

He led the way to a mass of huge rocks that

lay at some distance, heaped in confusion as though by some convulsion of nature. There were many crevices here that offered secure hiding places, and the travellers settled themselves under cover and waited for the storm to break.

They had not long to wait. With a roar and a rush the gale swept down the mountain passes. Against its terrific power it seemed as though nothing could stand. Had they been in the open, they would have been blown away like so many leaves.

Then came the rain, came in torrents, came as though, in the picturesque phrase of Alam, the sky had indeed broken. Its roar among the rocks about them sounded like thunder. In a moment, despite their protection, they were deluged with the waters that sought out every crack and crevice.

The flood surged down the defile in which the cars had been left like the waters from a broken dam. From the cliffs above the cars, they could hear it falling like a cataract. Would the ropes hold? Could the boulders they had wedged against the sides of the cars withstand that rushing flood?

At first they tried to encourage each other, but their voices could not be heard in that terrible pandemonium. Don reached out and clasped Teddy's hand, and the contact brought comfort to both of them.

The rain continued with unabated fury. All cowered there in the darkness, each one busy with his own gloomy thoughts. Perhaps the cars were already at the bottom of the chasm, having carried with them all their hopes of safety. If this had happened—they did not dare let their thoughts rest on what that would mean to them.

The others in the party envied Alam and Abdullah. They, no doubt, wrapped in their fatalism, had long since ceased to worry. They were in the hands of Allah. If Allah decreed that they should live, it was well. If Allah decreed that they should die, it was well. The hour of their death had been fixed long before. Nothing could hasten it, nothing retard it. Why then fret their souls about it?

But the Americans had not been nurtured on that philosophy, comforting and soothing as it sometimes was. Their instinct was to struggle, to defy death, to fight till the last gasp. And their hearts were torn with anxiety and apprehension, as the war of the elements continued.

Suddenly, close at hand, there came a tremendous crash.

"It's the cars!" cried Teddy. "They've gone over the cliffs!"

CHAPTER XVIII

THE MYSTERIOUS MOUNDS

"Not so bad as that, I hope!" exclaimed Don, an awful sinking at his heart. "If the cars have gone over the cliff——"

He did not finish, for to him as to all the members of the party the same fear had come. That crash sounded like the knell of doom.

After hours of torture, the storm at last abated. And when they crept back to their encampment they scarcely dared look.

A shout of infinite joy and relief went up from all as their eyes fell on the cars, standing not where they had been left, but still standing.

How severely the cars had felt the power of the storm was apparent at a glance. The ropes that had held one of them to the cliff had been torn from the fastenings and the car itself had been forced by the power of wind and water to within a few inches of the edge of the chasm. Had the storm continued a little longer, it would inevitably have fallen into the abyss.

The ropes of the other cars had also yielded, and the machines were standing athwart the path instead of parallel with it. The heavy boulders had been pushed along with them, but had at least prevented the cars from being dashed to destruction.

Not more than twenty feet behind the cars was

a great tear in the cliff where tons of rock had been loosened by the storm and had plunged into the chasm. This was the explanation of the thunderous crash they had heard.

"A mighty close call," muttered Don.

"But a miss is as good as a mile," said Teddy, trying to speak lightly.

It was with profoundly lightened hearts that the travellers set about getting breakfast. By this time their appetites had reasserted themselves and all did full justice to the meal.

They did not dare start too soon on those slippery paths, for skidding would be attended by the gravest danger. So they waited till the sun had risen and dried the roads.

"Gee!" exclaimed Don, when at last he and Brick climbed into their car to resume their journey, "this old driver's seat certainly looks good to me. Last night I was afraid that I was never going to sit in it again."

"Same here," agreed Brick. "Suppose at this moment all these cars were a mere mass of junk in that deep chasm."

"In that case we'd probably never see civilisation again," replied Don soberly. "It's a cinch that we couldn't make our way on foot in this desert. Our bones would form part of the many collections we've seen since we started on this trip."

"And all my hopes of seeing my father again would have gone glimmering," said Brick. "It gives me the shivers to think of it. And there we were like idiots rejoicing when we heard the rain was coming."

"That's because we didn't know what rain in the Sahara is like," returned Don. "I haven't any use for sandstorms, but as between the two, give me the sandstorm every time."

Most of the time the path wound upwards, but at times it sloped suddenly downwards and widened out into a broad plateau. In either case, travelling was difficult, and those at the wheel had to drive with the greatest caution.

It was evident that the time was near at hand when the cars would have to be abandoned altogether and the party proceed on foot. It was not a pleasant outlook, for all knew that it would immensely multiply the difficulties and dangers of the trip.

Because the air had been greatly cooled by the storm, it was possible to prolong the morning stretch, and it was fully noon before the usual midday halt was made.

No one had had any sleep the night before, and as soon as the meal was dispatched all, except Abdullah, whose turn it was to stand guard, sought their blankets for a long rest.

Ordinarily Don would have slept as soon as he had stretched his length on the ground. But to-day sleep was denied him. He changed his position again and again in the hope of wooing the drowsy god, but in vain. His nerves were too strained, his mind too active.

All that morning Brick had been talking to him about his father. The possibility that he was near him made it difficult for the lad to think or talk of anything else. Don had listened sympathetically, but the conversation had opened again the old wound, and now the thought of his own family, their mysterious fate, their possible sufferings, kept racing through his mind. Oh, if he could only find them, listen once more to their voices, look once more into their faces, hear them speak his name!

At last, to turn the current of his thoughts, which seemed as though they would drive him crazy, he rose softly, so as not to disturb the sleepers, and stole on tiptoe out of the tent. He had no definite purpose in mind, and vaguely thought that he would wander about for a while and finally get so weary that he could come back and get the sleep he craved and needed.

As he passed his Uncle Frank's car, he saw his field glasses lying on the seat, for the captain used them almost constantly, now that he was in this dangerous district. They were very powerful, and bore the name of a celebrated maker.

Don picked them up and slung the strap over his shoulder. He passed Abdullah, and nodded to him, telling him in a whisper that he was not going far and would keep in sight of the cars.

Sage and cactus bushes were growing about the place and at one point were so thick that Don had to push them aside to make his way through them. The next moment he recoiled, with a startled exclamation, for he had almost stepped off the brink of a precipice.

His surprise was the greater because there had been no inkling that there was any break in the level character of the plateau. Yet now he stood on the very brink of a cliff from which he could look down into a depression several miles wide, and so long that he could not see the end of it.

There was no verdure, unless that name could be applied to the coarse and stunted vegetation that showed in some parts of the broad expanse. Before him stretched an almost unbroken plain of amber sand, glittering in the rays of the Sahara sun.

Almost unbroken, but not quite. As Don looked, he noted little hillocks that broke the monotonous flatness of the plain. And they were not scattered at random, but had almost the regularity of a geometrical figure.

At first the thought flashed through his mind that it was of human construction. Intelligence seemed to be indicated by the almost circular shape. Could it be that it was a rude native fortification of some kind?

He unslung the field glasses from his shoulder, and, lying flat on the ground almost at the edge of the cliff, he scanned the valley for any sign of human life. There was none. There were no date palms in sight, nothing that indicated one of the oases where a little group of nomads would locate. Everything was bare, silent and desolate.

Having satisfied himself on that point, he turned his attention again to the little mounds that had at first stirred his curiosity. The glasses brought them near, and he was more impressed than ever with their peculiarities.

Now he discovered that what at first had seemed one circle had resolved itself into three. There were that many concentric rings, lying one within the other. At intervals in those rings were mounds that he could now see were many feet in height.

He knew that he had stumbled on something interesting and probably important, but for the life of him he could not figure out what.

Circles! Where had he heard talk of circles? Fragments of conversation in which the word had occurred came floating back to him, and he tried to piece them into a coherent whole. Circles! Then suddenly a thought came to him that filled him with wild excitement. Could it be possible?

He jumped to his feet and raced back to the little encampment. Abdullah sprang up and looked at him in alarm and then behind him, as though he expected to see a gang of Tuaregs at his heels.

"It's all right, Abdullah!" panted Don. "Nothing to worry about!"

He pulled aside the flap of the tent shared by the captain and the professor. He shook the latter by the shoulder.

"What is it?" asked Amos Bruce, yawning sleepily.

"I didn't want to disturb you, Uncle Amos," panted Don. "But I thought you'd want to know. I think I've found the Cemetery of the Elephants!"

There was no sleepiness now in the eyes of Professor Bruce. He leaped to his feet with a quickness alien to his placid nature.

"The Cemetery of the Elephants!" he cried. "What makes you think that?"

Don told him, his words tumbling over each other in his excitement.

The captain, who had been awakened by the hubbub, listened with almost as much avidity as the professor. Then both hurried with Don to the edge of the cliff. The glasses were again called into use and they studied the odd circles with the greatest care and the keenest interest.

"I think Don's right," declared the professor. "Those mounds seem to answer all the requirements of the old tradition. But we will soon find out."

They hurried back to the cars and got some spades and picks. The cars could not be left alone, and the party had to be divided. The captain and the professor took Don and Alam along with them to find access to the valley, while Brick and Abdullah stood guard over the camp.

Brick was in a state of intense excitement, and the hours had never seemed to drag so much as they did while he was awaiting the return of the others. Would it prove only a false hope? Or had Don really fallen upon a great discovery?

The sun was setting and darkness rapidly gathering when Brick gave a shout.

"Here they come!" he cried. "And, by crickey, see what they've got with them!"

Into the open came the party, weary but triumphant. In the hands of each was a great gleaming tusk of ivory!

CHAPTER XIX

A WONDERFUL DISCOVERY

WITH a wild hurrah Brick ran forward.

"So you were right, were you?" cried the boy. "That really was the Cemetery of the Elephants?"

"Here are the proofs of it," replied Don, relinquishing into Brick's eager hands the ivory tusk he carried.

"It's one of the most wonderful discoveries of the century!" affirmed Professor Bruce. "It will create a furore in the scientific world when it becomes known. This alone would have amply repaid me for my trip to this part of the world."

"To say nothing of the financial value of the discovery," put in the captain. "The ivory alone in those mounds down there is worth many thousands of dollars. There are scores of the mounds, and each one of them must contain the skeleton of one of the elephants that went there to die at the time that the jungle was much closer to this district than it is now. We dug into four mounds, and in each one we came upon bones and tusks."

"I'm mighty glad you found the Cemetery of the Elephants!" exclaimed Brick to Don. "That's one object of the trip accomplished."

"It was merely by accident that I caught sight of the mounds," replied Don modestly.

"Yes," agreed the professor. "But it wasn't

accident that made you associate your glimpse of them with the Cemetery of the Elephants. Anyone less keen might have glanced idly at them, let it go at that, and not even thought of mentioning it. No, the discovery rightly falls to you, and when I reveal the matter to the world I'll see that you get full credit for it."

For the rest of that afternoon there was jubilation in the camp. Professor Bruce especially was in the seventh heaven of delight. It seemed to him at times that he must be in a dream. But the sight of the ivory tusks proved that it was far more substantial than any dream.

"Well, now that we've made the find, what are we going to do about it?" asked Captain Sturdy later on, as they sat at their evening meal.

"I know what I'd like to do," replied the professor. "If we had nothing more important on hand "— he glanced kindly at Brick—"I'd like to settle right down here, explore every feature of the phenomenon and write my treatise about it right on the spot. But all that must wait until we've done all we can to rescue Mr. Allison."

Brick looked at him gratefully.

"And after that?" asked Don inquiringly.

"After that," declared the professor, "we'll make a careful map of this place, get its exact latitude and longitude, and then return to Tuggurt. There we'll organise a big expedition, bring along some motor trucks made on the same principle as these cars, exhume the ivory, and have it sent to America. Some of the tusks we'll give to museums and scientific societies. The rest we'll dispose of for what they will bring. And we'll divide what profit we make among all the members of the expedition. And when I say that, I mean that you, Alam, and you, Abdullah, shall share and share alike with the rest. You're taking your part of the risks of this expedition, and it's only fair that you should share in the gains."

Abdullah grinned from ear to ear, and Alam bowed with grave dignity.

"The master is generous," he said.

"Not at all," disclaimed the professor. "Only fair."

It was really more than fair, for it was going beyond custom, and the Arabs were already being well paid for their services. But the professor, and the captain as well, were accustomed to act on a broad-gauge scale.

"Well, leaving that matter for the present," said the captain, "let's come to a decision on the subject of the cars. We've gone just about as far as we can go with them, and during most of the rest of the time we're in these wilds we'll have to go on foot."

Don and Brick looked at each other in dismay.

"I've known for the last day or two that we'd have to do it," said Captain Sturdy, addressing himself especially to Don. "And I've been looking around, as we came along, to find a good place in which to hide the cars. But I've seen nothing that suited me until to-day. That's another thing for which we're indebted to you, Don."

"I don't see where I've had anything to do with it," replied Don, in some surprise.

"Indirectly, of course," replied his uncle. "But if

we hadn't gone down into this valley as a result
of your discovery, we wouldn't have seen the place
I'm referring to."

"So you found a cave down there?" asked Brick.

"One that seemed to be made for us," was the
reply. "Plenty large enough to hold all the cars,
and so hidden naturally by sage brush and cactus
that it was only when I accidentally fell and slid
through some of the bushes that I discovered it."

"Perhaps whatever people there are in this district
know of it too," suggested Don, a little uneasily.

"Possible, of course," assented the captain. "But
there were no traces of human habitation, no ashes
from fires or anything of that kind to indicate that
it had been visited for years. The valley is absolutely
a desert, without date trees or water, and there's no
inducement for anyone to go into it."

"There's one other thing," put in the professor,
"that would keep the tribesmen away from it, and
that is the fact that the elephants' tombs are there.
There's an old tradition that the ghosts of the
elephants walk at night. Probably people avoid the
place as they would the plague."

"So much the better for our purpose," laughed
Don. "This is one of the times when I give three
cheers for superstition."

"We'll get the cars down there the first thing in
the morning," decided Captain Sturdy.

"We'll have to be mighty careful in doing it, for
the slope is steep, but I'm sure we can make it all
right!" exclaimed Don joyously.

As soon as the first streaks of dawn showed on
the horizon the travellers snatched a hurried break-

fast and started the cars on what was to be their last trip for some time to come. Great care was necessary in making the descent, but at last the cars came to a stop at the place the captain indicated.

He had not exaggerated the advantages of the cave as a hiding place, for the boys looked for it in vain until the captain took the lead and pushed aside the bushes that concealed the opening.

By the aid of their flashlights, they explored the place, which was a natural opening into a beetling cliff. It ranged in width from twenty to thirty feet, and ran in for sixty feet or more. It was admirably adapted, not only for concealment, but also, in case of discovery, for defence, as a few determined men by the aid of boulders that stood near and could easily be gathered in time of need, could stand off assailants many times their number.

No track of man or beast could be discovered in the vicinity or on the floor of the cave, which looked as though it were covered with the dust of ages.

"What do you think of it?" asked Captain Sturdy of the boys.

"Fine!" declared Brick.

"Dandy!" pronounced Don. "It couldn't be better for our purpose. But it makes me feel bad to have to leave the cars. They seem like old friends."

"And mighty good friends they've been to us," replied his uncle. "But we're up against hard necessity, and we have to yield to it. I hope we'll be in them again soon, and with Mr. Allison on one of the front seats."

It was a hard problem to decide what to take from the cars and what to leave behind. The searchers did not want to burden themselves too heavily, and yet they had to take along with them the absolutely necessary things they required. First among these, of course, came food and water, their guns and ammunition. These alone would prove heavy burdens in that hot climate. What would they not have given to have had a camel at their disposal!

The machine-guns were abandoned with the utmost reluctance. One of them in case of need might be worth a dozen men. They looked at them longingly, but had to give up the idea on account of their weight.

But they did add to their ammunition a dozen hand grenades of the most powerful kind. At close range, they were terribly effective weapons. And nobody knew how soon they might have to use them.

At last their preparations were completed, and they set out with burdened shoulders, and also with burdened hearts. For none of them was under any delusion as to the added danger that confronted them now that they were on foot. Against mounted enemies they would be at a special disadvantage. They could neither pursue them nor run away from them.

Nor could they travel as fast and as far in their search for Mr. Allison. They could only make a few miles a day, and would have to stop frequently for rest. The greater part of their travelling would have to be done very early in the morning and very late in the afternoon and evening.

For these disadvantages, however, there were

some compensations. On foot, they would not be so conspicuous to prying eyes as though they were in the cars. And then, too, they could go where cars could not. Also, they could move more noiselessly.

Before they started, the captain distributed some kola nuts among them.

"We'll have to be as sparing with the water as possible," he said, "and to some extent these will take the place of it. When you are very thirsty, put one of these in your mouth and keep it there. It's surprising how they satisfy thirst."

They had gone several miles, and their loads were becoming intolerably heavy, when suddenly Don, who was in advance, made a gesture and dropped flat on the ground.

Trusting in Don's judgment, the others instantly did the same.

CHAPTER XX

TAKEN BY SURPRISE

THE others dragged themselves along the ground until they were close beside Don. At his indication, they lifted their heads a trifle above a little ridge covered with mimosa scrub that offered them some protection from discovery.

Before them was a clump of palm trees, near which was a small mud-walled house. Beneath the shade of the trees sat three natives, while their camels, tethered by long ropes, grazed on the scanty herbage that the place afforded.

The captain unslung his field glasses and made a prolonged examination of the objects that had brought them to the sudden halt.

"What do you think of them, Alam?" asked Captain Sturdy in a low voice, as he handed the glasses to the guide, crouching beside him.

Alam took a long look.

"Men of the mountains," he answered. "Tuaregs, demanders of tribute."

"I thought as much," muttered the captain. "That seems to be the chief occupation in these parts. In our country we call them thieves. They're pretty rough looking specimens."

He passed the glasses to the others, and they all studied the first men they had seen for many days. The glasses came last to Brick, who, almost as soon as his eyes fell on the strangers gave a startled exclamation.

"There is one of the men who made the raid on our caravan and carried off my father!" he exclaimed. "That one with the broken nose, over at the right."

"Are you sure?" inquired Don, greatly excited, though he kept his voice low.

"Positive," replied Teddy. "I saw him plainly at the time, and I noticed that his nose was broken."

"That's the best news I've heard for some time," said the captain. "I think we'll start proceedings right away."

The man in question was smoking a narghile, one of the long pipes with a deep bowl common among the desert people.

The captain drew his rifle and took careful aim.

"Think well, Frank," counselled the professor, laying his hand on the captain's arm. "We don't want to do any killing and stir up the natives against us if it can be avoided."

"Don't worry, Amos," returned the captain. "I'm not going to kill anyone. But I'm going to give that party the surprise of their lives. That broken-nosed fellow is going to have a scare thrown into him.

"The moment I fire," he commanded, "the rest of you jump up and rush with me at the gang. If I figure rightly, they'll make a break for the house. The door seems to be the only place they can fire from, for I don't see any windows. We'll surround the house on the other three sides and then we can come to a parley with them. Be ready now. Don," he said suddenly, "you are a good enough shot now to do the business. Take your rifle and aim at the fellow's pipe."

Don, his face shining with delight, took careful aim. The bowl of the pipe was shattered to pieces.

There was a howl of surprise and fright, and at the same instant Don's party broke into view, running at top speed, shouting and waving their rifles.

For a moment the Tuaregs stood as though paralysed. Then they rushed pell-mell into the house and slammed the door, and the pursuers could hear the dropping of a heavy bar to secure it.

"Around to the sides!" commanded the captain, and was obeyed in a twinkling.

The Americans and the Arabs stood there, panting and waiting for what was to come next. To the hubbub caused by the irruption into the house had succeeded a dead silence, during which Teddy whispered to Don:

"Gee, but that was a dandy shot! Wish I could do as well."

The captain beckoned to Alam.

"Our little surprise seems to have been a success so far," he said. "Now here's where you come in. Call out to those fellows and tell them that we mean them no harm, even if we have introduced ourselves rather abruptly. If they behave themselves and give us the information we want, they will shortly be allowed to go where they wish. But there must be no treachery and no falsehood, or it will go hard with them. Start in with that and see what they say. But don't get in range of the door."

Alam went to the corner of the house and called out the Arab equivalent of the American: "Hallo, in there!"

There was no answer at first, and he repeated the call twice. Then a sullen voice, trembling with rage and perhaps with fear, responded:

"Who are you? What do you want?"

"We are peaceful travellers," replied Alam. "We have no thought of evil in our hearts. We want to talk with you and find out things that perhaps you know. Afterwards you may go in peace."

"And suppose we refuse to tell you?" came the voice.

"It will not be well to refuse," replied Alam. "Allah has delivered you into our hands. We are two to your one. And you have seen how the Feringhee can shoot. He could have killed you as easily as he smashed your pipe. But his heart is good, and he does not wish your hurt."

He ceased, and there was the sound of a hurried conference within.

"I guess they'll think it wise to come to terms," commented Don.

"If they agree to come out, tell them that they must come out without their weapons, one at a time, and they must agree to permit themselves to be bound," ordered the captain. "If they tell us the truth, they will be released. If they kick at this condition, tell them that the gun that broke the pipe is still ready for business. And," he added to Don, "the boy who shot it is right at hand."

A moment later a call came from within.

"We will come out," said the same voice as before, evidently that of the leader.

"It is well," replied Alam, and announced the further stipulations laid down by the captain. There was some demur at these, but Alam's mention of Don's rifle proved effective.

The door was thrown open, and the first man appeared. The captain held him under his levelled rifle, while Don and Brick tied his hands and ordered him to sit down on the ground. The same process was carried out with the others.

"So far, so good," remarked Don, as his uncle laid his rifle aside.

"Now, let's see if we can get them to talk. Find out who is the leader, Alam," ordered Captain Sturdy.

Alam, after a moment's inquiry, pointed to the man with the broken nose, a villainous-looking fellow even apart from that deformity.

"It is he," announced Alam.

"Good!" exclaimed the captain. "Now, Alam, ask him this: 'Where is the Feringhee you carried off into captivity?'"

CHAPTER XXI

THE CONFESSION

ALAM shot the question at the captive with the same rapidity which the captain had imparted to it.

The man started violently as he grasped its import. His companions were also agitated. It was evident that the arrow shot at a venture had gone home. But the next moment the sullen eyes of the leader became expressionless, and he shook his head.

"I do not know what you mean," he said.

But the momentary disturbance that the question had caused him had not been lost on the Americans.

"Tell him that his heart is double," Don's uncle directed Alam. "Tell him that the Feringhee is sure that he is not telling the truth. It would be better to speak with a straight tongue unless he wishes to be gathered to his fathers."

Alam translated this injunction, but it seemed to have no effect. The man stubbornly persisted in his denial. He knew enough of the white man's ways to feel sure that he would not be killed in cold blood.

While the captain stood pondering his next act, Alam's eyes rested on the youngest and slightest of the prisoners. The man gave an almost imperceptible sign that had an instantaneous effect on the guide, who hesitated a moment and then made a similar sign in return.

"I confess I'm up a tree, Amos," the captain said, turning to Professor Bruce. "I feel morally certain that this fellow is lying. I suppose I could apply some third-degree methods, but I don't like to do that except as a last resort."

"Perhaps some of the others will tell you something," suggested Don. "They don't look quite as hardened as their leader. Suppose you try them, and come back to this fellow if you have to."

Captain Sturdy was about to adopt the suggestion when Alam interposed.

"Will the master permit me to make a suggestion?" he asked.

Permission was given, and Alam unburdened himself. The youngest of the captives had given him a mystic sign of a secret Mohemmedan society of which both were members. It might simply have been meant to implore help in the present situation, but Alam had an impression it meant more than that. He felt that if the others were removed out of earshot he could talk freely with the man in question, and perhaps find out what they wanted to know.

"Go to it," said the captain, to whom the plan looked promising.

The two older captives were ordered to rise and go some little distance, where they remained under the guard of Don, Brick and Abdullah, while Alam engaged the other in an earnest conversation. Alam seemed to be pleading and threatening by turns, while the captive hesitated, begged and evaded.

At last Alam, with a look of satisfaction on his face, turned to the eagerly expectant group.

"He knows and he will tell," he announced.

"Good for you, Alam," commended the captain.

"But," continued Alam, "he asks that the other tribesmen be removed from sight within the house so that they may not gather from our words or from our faces what he is saying. Should they know that he confessed the truth, death might later be his portion."

"That's fair enough," agreed the captain, giving the necessary directions, and the men were driven into the house, Don and Abdullah standing guard at the door.

"Now," Captain Sturdy continued, using Alam as his spokesman, "do you know anything about the Feringhee that was captured in the raid?"

"Yes," was the reply.

At this response, Brick bent forward, all his soul in his eyes. Looking at the trembling boy, the captain scarcely dared to ask the next question. But he nerved himself to it.

"Is he alive?"

"He is alive."

There was a cry of frantic delight from Brick, and he burst into tears.

"There, there," said the professor, his own eyes moist, as he threw his arm over Teddy's shoulders. "I congratulate you, my dear boy. It's wonderful news."

"He's alive!" cried Brick enthusiastically. "He's alive! My own dear father is alive! All that I have on earth! I haven't any mother, you know," and again his frame shook with sobs.

The captain waited a minute or two to allow

Brick to gain control of himself and then proceeded with the questioning.

Now that the first step had been taken, the man made a clean breast of it. Mr. Allison had been carried off into captivity with the idea that it might be possible to secure a ransom for his release. The man had an impression that some negotiations were even then going on through some of the mysterious agencies that the desert folk relied on in such cases. In the meantime, it was to the captors' own interests that he should be kept alive and well, at any rate till it became unlikely that he would be ransomed. He had been compelled to work for his captors, but had not been brutally treated, and was in good health the last time the man had seen him, which was about a week before. All this came out bit by bit, by dint of repeated question.

It was balm to Teddy's sore heart. His father was alive and well! What else mattered? He already saw himself reunited to him.

But to the captain and the professor a great deal else mattered. The essential thing, of course, was that Mr. Allison was alive. But they were still a long way off from the rescue they contemplated. How was that to be effected?

Would the guide lead them to the place where the Feringhee was held in bondage? That was a different question. His people would kill him if they suspected that he had been instrumental in the release of the captive. No, he would not dare to do that. The revenge of the desert tribesmen was sure and swift. He did not want to die.

At last they reached a compromise. He would

lead them part of the way and give them accurate directions for the rest of the journey. Then he would take his camel and travel to Tuggurt and there await the return of the party. He was sick of a robber's life, and had long wished for a change. This was his chance, and he was willing to accept it. Alam would help him get some work that would give him a livelihood and the captain and the professor would see that he was liberally supplied with funds to give him a start.

Teddy had not waited to hear all this conversation, which mainly concerned his elders. He was bursting with impatience that Don, dear old Don, who had been so sympathetic, should hear the glorious news.

He approached the house over which Don was standing guard with Abdullah.

"Don," said Brick, in a voice he tried to make calm and ordinary in order to reveal nothing to the prisoners, "can you step here for a moment?"

"Sure thing," was the response.

One glance at Teddy's face was enough to tell the story.

Don grabbed him by the shoulder and hurried him out of earshot.

"Your father——" he began.

"Is alive!" cried Teddy. "Oh, Don, he's alive!"

CHAPTER XXII

FOLLOWING THE CLUE

"GLORY HALLELUJAH!" ejaculated Don, his joy almost equalling that of his friend. "Didn't I tell you that I had a hunch we'd find him all right? I'd rather hear that news, Brick, than get a million dollars."

"That's bully of you to say so, Don, and I'll never be able to tell you how thankful I am to you and to your uncles for all the sympathy and help you've given me. I only hope you'll have equal luck in the search for your parents."

"I hope so," returned Don, a swift pang stabbing his heart at the vagueness of his knowledge as to their whereabouts. "We'll take this as a good omen, anyway. Now the next thing is, to get your father out of the claws of these rascals."

At these words a cloud swept over Brick's face. "Oh, if only we can get to him! We must get to him!" he exclaimed.

How that was to be done was at that very moment being discussed by the boys' elders, who were mapping out the course of action to be followed. By their calculations, the place where Mr. Allison was being held captive could be reached, if they had luck, on the second day from the present one. By forced marches they might even get there by the night of the following day.

The hands of the young Arab were now freed

from bonds, though not without some misgivings on the part of the Americans. These were removed by Alam, who made the man swear on the Koran that he would keep his word. The guide was confident that the young man would not break that most sacred of oaths in the Mohammedan world.

While a hasty meal was being prepared previous to their setting out, the professor took the young Arab in hand and questioned him about the City of Brass.

The man was reluctant to talk about it at first, and professed to be ignorant of its exact location. Gradually, however, the professor elicited that there was a mysterious city that lay a little way off from the line of march that would have to be traversed on the way to Mr. Allison's place of bondage.

"Have you ever seen it or been in it?"

"No, Allah forbid! My life would pay the forfeit for such rashness. At times I have seen afar off what seemed to be the towers and pinnacles of a great city. But, Allah be praised, I was on foot at such times and swiftly turned my eyes in another direction. Has the Feringhee not heard that the gates are guarded by jinns and demons?"

Amos Bruce sighed at the superstition, but gently kept up his questioning. To all suggestions that the man should lead them to the spot the fellow returned a blank refusal. They might come in sight of it on their march, and if the Feringhee chose to look at it or investigate more closely, that was his own concern. But he would have no part in such impiety.

It developed, also, that the strange city lay in the

territory of a wild and fierce people, who would not allow anyone to go through their domain. It was a strange land, where even the water was bewitched. If any but the natives drank of it, they would be transformed into animals or reptiles.

There was no special promise of immediate results from this conversation, but the professor was mightily stirred by these revelations. Surely, where there was so much smoke there must be some fire. How he wished that he were at the head of an expedition numerous enough and strong enough to force its way through the mysterious land and determine once for all the truth or falsity of the tradition.

The meal was now ready, and Don and Abdullah were summoned to eat with the rest.

"I guess the captives are safe enough, tied as they are," remarked Don, as he came forward. "Anyway, we can watch the door of the house, if they should try to escape."

"They're sort of white elephants on our hands, anyway," observed the professor, in some perplexity. "What do you think we'd better do with them, Frank?"

"Keep our eyes on them 'till we come across Mr. Allison and then turn them loose," was the reply.

They ate hastily but heartily, for they contemplated a march that would last far into the night. Then, while the loads were being gathered up, the captain sent Abdullah to the house to bring out the prisoners.

When Abdullah reached the door he gave vent to

an expression of surprise and alarm and came hurrying back.

"What is it?" asked Don, looking up from his task of reloading a rifle.

"The men have gone!" replied Abdullah.

"Gone!" exclaimed the captain. "Impossible! They couldn't have got out of that door without our seeing them."

"They are gone," repeated the Arab.

Don and the others rushed to the house. The one room was empty. They looked at each other in bewilderment.

"A jinn must have helped them," suggested Abdullah.

But the hard-headed Americans were sceptical in the matter of jinns. They looked at the roof, which was intact. They searched every part of the room. When in the darkest corner Don uttered an exclamation.

"Here's the jinn that helped them in their getaway!" he ejaculated. "Here's a trap door leading to an underground passage. Why didn't we examine this room more closely? Now the birds have flown. But perhaps they haven't gone far."

Without an instant's hesitation, he lowered himself into the opening, his Uncle Frank close at his heels. They followed the passage, which proved to be a long one opening beyond a clump of bushes some distance beyond the palm trees. They looked in all directions but could see no trace of the fugitives. And once out of sight in that country so familiar to them, they might as well look for a needle in a haystack.

"They put one over on us that time," Don remarked grimly, as he and his uncle rejoined the party.

"I wouldn't have lost them for worlds," Captain Sturdy said. "And we haven't time to search for them, even as a forlorn hope. I didn't want them to have a chance to get back to their people and warn them of our coming."

"They don't know yet that we've found out anything about Mr. Allison," suggested the professor hopefully; "so they may not be in a great hurry to get back."

"No," said the captain, "but they know we're looking for him."

"And it will take them a good while to get free from the ropes," said Don. "Gee, I wish we'd tied their feet as well as their hands!"

"They will not want to go without their camels," observed Alam. "A man of the desert values his camel above all else. They will hide till we have gone and then come back for their beasts."

"That gives me an idea," cried Don. "We'll turn them loose and they'll wander off. It will probably take a long time to find them, and that may give us the start we need."

Abdullah untethered the animals and gave them a few smart blows that sent them away. Then the party hastened along on the long march that lay before them.

Fortune favoured them in the possession of the camel of their young prisoner, or, as they now regarded him, their guide, for they could pack on the brute the greater part of their loads and thus proceed in light marching order.

They did not underestimate the perils that lay before them, but their hearts were high with hope, for now they had a definite goal in view.

They made surprisingly good time. Their guide took them by the shortest cuts, and they went on till midnight, resting even then only a few hours and being on the road again at the first signs of dawn. Only when the sun was near the zenith did they stop for their midday meal at the edge of a broad plateau.

The professor had been absorbed in his thoughts, speaking but seldom and casting frequent glances towards the horizon. After dinner he took the field glasses, and, stretching himself out on the ground in the shadow of a mimosa bush, scanned the wide expanse.

Suddenly his glance became fixed. His hands trembled, as he called to his nephew.

"Take these glasses, Don," he directed. "Look over in that direction and tell me what you see."

Don did so, and instantly, his excitement was as great as that of the professor's.

"Great Scott, Uncle Amos!" he sputtered, "it isn't—it isn't the City of Brass!"

"What else?" asked Professor Bruce, in a voice he tried to keep calm.

There in the far distance were the turrets and towers and domes of what looked like a great city. It might have been Cairo or Alexandria, as far as size or magnificence was concerned.

"Uncle Frank! Brick!" yelled Don, in excitement. "Come here! Come here and look!"

Captain Sturdy and Teddy came hastily, followed by Alam and Abdullah. The two former were as excited as Don and his Uncle Amos when they, too, gazed on the wonderful scene.

"It can't—it can't possibly be a mirage, do you think?" asked the captain, in an awed voice.

"Not possible," was Professor Bruce's reply. "Nature is a great artist, but she doesn't make pictures like that. There's only one explanation. The City of Brass is not a myth, but a reality."

The professor offered the glasses to the Arabs also, but these stubbornly refused to use them. They guessed the cause of the agitation, and kept their eyes turned in another direction, making mystic signs designed to ward off evil spirits. Even though they were not on a camel's back, they were taking no chances.

"Oh, if we could go there!" sighed the professor.

"Not yet, but soon," replied the captain, with quiet determination. "We haven't time, and it's enough for this trip that we've located it. That in itself will set the scientific world buzzing. Later on—well, I've seldom set my mind on anything that I haven't realised sooner or later."

"Yes, but look below!" cried Don, who had the field glasses. "How would you cross that?"

All gazed down to what he pointed out—a wide, irregular split in the earth's surface, similar to the split into which Don had slipped during the sand-storm. But this split was much wider and deeper, and both ends were lost in the distance.

"Gee, what an opening!" cried Brick, as he gave a look through the glasses. "If you fell into that you'd never get out alive!"

"I guess that is what guards the City of Brass from all comers," answered Don. "You'd have to have an airship to get to it."

"We'll even get that if necessary," declared the captain, with determination. "But do you realise, Amos, that if we're in the vicinity of the City of Brass, we're probably not far from the Cave of Emeralds?"

"You're right," agreed the professor, with quickened animation. "They're linked together in the tradition. You remember the party that went out from the city with the store of emeralds and didn't return? The men themselves perished, but the emeralds didn't. They're still in existence somewhere."

They tore themselves away with reluctance from the marvellous vision. But time was pressing and their guide was getting restless. He had nearly fulfilled his bargain and was about to leave them. They were now near the goal of their search. They might reach it even that night. A little later, with careful directions for the remainder of their march, the young Arab mounted his camel, left them, and took up his long journey to Tuggurt.

The Americans were keyed up now to the highest pitch. They examined their arms to see that they were in good condition, and, with Alam and Abdullah, pressed on until, just before dark, they came upon the edge of what seemed a small settlement that answered to the description given them by the guide.

They spread out in a long line, and with the stealth of Indians wormed their way along, crouching low and taking advantage of scrubs and bushes for cover.

An evening hush hung over the place, which seemed to have about a score of scattered houses, each surrounded by a small patch of ground.

Suddenly Don's heart gave a leap. He saw a little way before him the figure of a man working in one of the gardens some distance from a low, mud-walled house. He wore only a shirt and trousers and sandals. His hair was long and unkempt, and from a side view his face seemed covered with beard.

But his figure was not that of an Arab, and as he turned in Don's direction the latter saw that it was not an Arab's face.

Don crept as near as he could without emerging from cover.

"Mr. Allison!" he called.

CHAPTER XXIII

PURSUED

THE man started violently and turned in astonishment.

"Who is calling me?" he exclaimed.

"A friend," answered Don, pushing aside the

bushes far enough to reveal his face. "I'm one of a party who have come to rescue you."

"Thank God!" exclaimed the man, with a strong effort getting a grip on himself. "I had almost given up hope."

"Stay where you are and go on with your work while I get my friends together," counselled Don.

"Yes, but hurry," was the answer, as the man looked apprehensively around. "The natives are at supper now, but they will soon be out of doors again."

Don drew back and hurriedly found his companions.

"I've found him!" he announced. "Mr. Allison! He's over behind that clump of bushes, working in a garden. He knows we're here, and he's ready the minute we give the word."

"My father!" exclaimed Brick, and started to rush forward, but the others restrained him.

"Steady, steady now," warned the captain, putting his hand on the boy's arm. "You'll be with him in a minute."

They went swiftly and cautiously towards the place that Don indicated. Mr. Allison had, with apparent indifference, worked his way down close to the line of bushes.

They were about to call to him when their hearts leaped in consternation as they saw a man come out of the nearest house and look about him. He started to come towards the captive, but then, as though a second glance had reassured him that the prisoner was working hard, he halted, slowly retraced his steps to the house, and entered it.

Now was their moment, and they grasped it instantly.

"Come," called the captain in a voice just loud enough to carry.

Mr. Allison gave one last quick look around and then sprang through the bushes. The next instant Teddy had his arms about him.

"Father, Father!" he cried. "I thought I was never going to see you again!"

"Teddy! You here? My dear, dear boy!"

Mr. Allison fell on his knees beside his son and folded him in his arms.

The rest of the party, with eyes suspiciously wet, turned their backs for a moment, respecting that first sacred moment of reunion of father and son. But only for a moment. For time was pressing, and they were all in deadly peril.

"Hustle's the word now," said the captain. "Every instant is precious. Thank heaven it's nearly dark. But we'll have to get away from this place on the jump. Alam, it's up to you now. You've got the eyes of a cat. Get us out of this quickly. You lead the way, and we'll keep up with you."

Alam set off at a rapid gait, and the rest followed, Mr. Allison keeping tight hold of Teddy's hand.

No time was wasted in speech. They needed all their breath, and silence also was necessary.

Hours passed, and every muscle was sore and aching, but they kept on, close on the heels of the tireless Alam, until at last, shortly before midnight, the captain called a halt.

"We'll stay here for three hours," he announced, "and be up and away again before dawn. And now,

Mr. Allison, before we turn in I want to shake your hand. We'll make fuller acquaintance later on."

"I can never thank you all enough," replied Mr. Allison fervently, grasping in turn the hand of each member of the party. "It was a wonderful thing for you who were strangers to me to risk your lives in trying to rescue me."

"We weren't strangers to Teddy, though," replied Don.

"And we grew so attached to the plucky youngster that we simply had to find his father for him," added the captain. "We tried to interest the French and American authorities in your case, and we did interest them. But there is so much red tape connected with the matter that we finally decided to come ourselves."

"It was a magnificent thing to do," affirmed Mr. Allison. "I only hope that the doing of it won't prove serious to you."

"Do you think they'll pursue us?" asked Don.

"I'm afraid they will," was the answer. "Luckily many of the tribe are away on a marauding expedition. But there are enough left to give us a lot of trouble. I hope you have a gun for me."

"I brought an extra one along with that in mind," replied the captain. "From what I've heard from Teddy, I know that you know how to use it."

"He's a dead shot," declared Teddy proudly.

"It's a mighty fortunate thing that you came upon me just at the edge of dark," said Mr. Allison. "That's given us hours that we wouldn't otherwise have had. It was probably some time after we had started that they discovered my absence. Even then, they wouldn't have been especially suspicious for a time, for I was free to go about the settlement, and they'd have thought that I'd turn up later. They knew I hadn't a chance in the world of getting away from there alone and on foot, and probably the thought of a rescue party hadn't entered their minds. But by this time, of course, they know that something is up, and they'll probably be after us the first thing in the morning."

"Just one more question before we take our forty winks," said the captain. "Do you still have the map that you were depending on to find the Cave of Emeralds?"

A look of chagrin came into Mr. Allison's face.

"No," he replied. "It was taken from me by my captors. But I know we must be somewhere in the vicinity of the cave. I'd studied the map so long and hard that I think I can reproduce it from memory as soon as we have time. When daylight comes, I think I can at least indicate the general direction in which the cave lies."

"Good!" exclaimed Don. "Once throw these beggars off the track, or beat them off, if they attack us, and we'll get after the treasure cave, shan't we, Uncle Frank?"

"Yes. But now we'd better stretch out and get what rest we may."

Three hours later Alam awakened them, and they went on determined to reach their cars by night if possible. Once in those and fairly on their road, they could bid defiance to their foes. And having outdistanced these, they might start the search for the Cave of Emeralds.

For several hours they made rapid time. They passed a cave on one of the plateaus on which the captain looked with the appreciative eye of a military man.

"A capital place for defence," he muttered to himself.

They had got but a few yards farther on when Alam suddenly stopped and sniffed the air.

"What is it, Alam?" asked Don quickly.

"The smell of camels is in the air," was the reply. "There is a caravan in front of us, and coming this way."

The thought of the rascally Arabs from Tuggurt flashed through the minds of all. At the same moment they heard behind them, though evidently some distance off, the sound of galloping, and a rifle shot that sounded like a signal.

They looked at each other in consternation. Certain enemies back of them, probably enemies in front of them! They were caught between two fires!

CHAPTER XXIV

AGAINST HEAVY ODDS

THE captain at once took the lead. His plan was framed like lightning.

"Back to the cave," he commanded. "Quick! It's our only chance."

They rushed back to the cave they had passed a few moments before. It was a deep, roomy place with a narrow aperture. There were a number of heavy boulders scattered about, and these they piled into a rude breastwork, behind which all crouched and waited.

There was a bare chance, the captain figured, that the hostile parties in the haste of pursuit might pass the aperture without noting it. If not, they must defend themselves as best they could.

It seemed as though his hope was about to be realised when a troop of a dozen fierce-looking nomads, mounted on shaggy camels, passed the cave with scarcely a glance, their eyes bent on the road ahead. Mr. Allison recognised them at once as coming from the settlement from which he had escaped.

"I was sure they'd be after us," he murmured, as he gripped his rifle tightly. "But they'll never take me alive."

"They've gone on now," exulted the professor.

"They'll probably keep up the pursuit for hours before they turn back."

But Alam shook his head.

"They will be back," he prophesied. "They will soon find that our trail has stopped."

"Then, too, they'll meet those other fellows farther on, and they'll tell them that nobody got by them," said Teddy.

"Possibly they'll have a fight among themselves, and kill each other off like the Kilkenny cats," suggested Don hopefully.

But the captain had no such comfort in his thoughts.

"Not likely," he said. "They're birds of a feather, and they'll unite in a common hope of plunder. They may fight over the spoils after they get them, if they do, but not before."

"It's a kind of grim joke on them that there won't be any spoils to speak of," remarked the professor. "Those Tuggurt rascals, if that's who they are, probably think that by this time we've found the emeralds. But they'll get left."

"It will be a joke," agreed Don. "But if we're dead before it's sprung on them, we won't get much enjoyment out of it."

Before long they heard a hubbub of excited voices.

"They've met!" exclaimed Teddy.

"And they guess that we're somewhere near by," remarked Don. "They can't help seeing this cave when they look for it. I guess we're in for a fight."

The captain disposed his party to the best advantage behind the boulders, each one with his rifle thrust between some crevice that commanded a wide section of the space in front.

Into sight came a much larger party than the Americans had seen before, and well up towards the front rode the man with a scar.

"Our old friend, Gaza el Beno," muttered the captain. "If it's the last thing I do, that rascal will have more scars than one before this day is over."

The sharp eyes of the Mohammedans darted from side to side, and an exclamation from one of them showed that the retreat in the cave had been discovered.

"It's all up," remarked Don grimly.

"We'll get in the first blow, however," replied his Uncle Frank. "I'd better do the shooting this time, Don, though you did wonders when you broke that fellow's pipe."

He took careful aim and fired. The rein that Gaza el Beno held was whipped from his hand, and the shock nearly hurled him from the back of his camel.

A wild yell rose from the crowd and there followed a mad scattering for a place of safety. In a moment all the Mohammedans had disappeared.

"Just a little object lesson," remarked the captain. "They may not love us for it, but it may make them respect us. I don't want to hurt the beggars, unless they make us do so."

"Wonderful shooting," remarked Mr. Allison appreciatively.

There was profound silence for at least half an hour. Don and Brick began to hope that the attacking party had retired for good, but their more experienced elders had no such delusion.

At last there came a call from without.

"Answer it, Alam," the captain commanded.

Alam obeyed, and there was a brief interchange, which resulted in an Arab appearing in front of the cave carrying a white flag, which Alam had assured him would be respected.

"Find out what he wants, Alam," directed the captain.

"He complains that, though they had nothing but the most peaceful intentions towards everybody, we fired on his party and so made them our enemies," Alam reported, after a colloquy.

"How sweet of them," whispered Don, giving Brick a nudge in the ribs.

"But now that it is war," Alam went on, "they call on us to surrender. If we do this without further firing, they will not kill us but will only make slaves of us."

"And if we don't agree?"

"Then they will kill us and send us to the flames of Eblis. They are many, and they know that we are few."

"I see," said the captain. "Now tell him this. The Feringhees want nothing but to go in peace. The bullet that snapped the rein from the rider's hand could just as well have been sent through the rider's brain, if the Feringhee had so willed. If you attack them, there will be much wailing of widows in the tents for their men who will never return. If, however, you will swear on the Koran to let the Feringhees go in peace, all will be well."

Alam delivered the message and the herald withdrew. A few minutes later there was a spattering of bullets against the rocks.

"That's their answer," remarked Don. "It's the one we could have expected, I guess. They think that they've got us in a trap and they know they outnumber us. But we'll beat them yet!" he added confidently.

"We must husband our ammunition and trust they'll use up theirs," the captain said. "They're wasteful beggars and shoot at random. We must make every shot tell. Mr. Allison, Don and I as the best shots here, will do the firing unless it comes to close quarters, when we'll all join in. Shoot to wound but not to kill, if you can help it. We can put a man out of action one way as well as another. Aim at leg or arm or shoulder."

Soon every bush and boulder and sand ridge seemed alive with enemies. Their bullets rained like hail on the bulwark of the defenders.

Only occasionally did a bark come from the rifle of Don, the captain, or Mr. Allison. But every one had a target in some arm or leg when an Arab, in order to fire, exposed himself, and every bullet found its mark. Before long half a dozen of the attacking party were put out of the fight.

Then an order was shouted, and in a moment the space before the cave was again clear of foes.

"Guess they've got enough!" exulted Don.

"No," replied the captain. "They simply see they're whipped if they keep this up, and they're getting ready for a grand rush to try to wipe us out at one fell swoop."

There was another hour of tense waiting. Then the captain's prophecy was fulfilled.

With a wild yell the Arabs, appearing suddenly as though they had sprung from the ground, rushed at the cave from both sides, shooting as they came.

This time the attacking party threw prudence to the winds. There was no hunting for cover. Every man clambered up to the breastworks, tore at the boulders, and tried to dislodge them or climb over them.

"Fire!" shouted the captain, setting the example.

A rain of bullets poured from the defenders' rifles and several of the Arabs fell back wounded. But the rest kept on undauntedly.

Gaza el Beno was among the foremost, fighting savagely. He pulled himself up on the top of the breastwork and aimed a blow with his clubbed rifle at the professor's head. But before the blow could fall, Don had sent a bullet through his arm, and the rifle fell clattering from his fingers while he himself pitched in a huddled heap outside.

The fall of their leader disconcerted the Arabs, and another volley completed their discomfiture. They withdrew sullenly, still sending scattering shots.

Suddenly a ridge of fire ran along Don's left arm. It was like the searing of a red-hot iron!

CHAPTER XXV

GREAT NEWS FOR DON

"WHAT is it?" cried the captain, in alarm, as he saw Don's face whiten.

"Guess I got one of those bullets," replied Don, trying to smile.

With an exclamation of consternation the captain, aided by the equally anxious professor, rolled up Don's sleeve, while the rest of the party gathered anxiously round.

An angry red ridge showed itself along the upper part of the arm. The captain, an expert in wounds, examined it carefully, and then an expression of relief came into his face.

"I'm thankful it's no worse!" he exclaimed. "The bullet ran along it, but didn't go in. You'll have a mighty sore arm for a day or two, lad, but that's all."

The arm was treated with soothing emollients and bandaged.

"Lucky that arm wasn't hurt till you put Gaza el Beno out of business," said Teddy. "You did that just in time, Don."

"I said that I'd leave my mark on him to-day, but yours will do instead," remarked Captain Sturdy.

There was little probability that another attack would come for some hours, so, though guards were posted and a strict watch kept, the rest of the party could relax a little.

"They will come again at nightfall," prophesied Alam.

A meal was hastily prepared, of which all partook heartily, not only because they were hungry but in order that they should be fortified for what might still await them.

Don and Brick lingered longer than the others, but had nearly finished when the latter, looking around, exclaimed:

"What has become of Abdullah?"

"He was here a few minutes ago," replied Don, scanning the various members of the party. "I saw him near the back of the cave."

"He isn't there now," said Brick, with a touch of anxiety. "Could anything have happened to him?"

The next moment Abdullah himself appeared.

Don intercepted him. The captain, the professor and Mr. Allison were talking earnestly with Alam at the entrance to the cave.

"Where have you been, Abdullah?" Don asked. "We were getting worried about you."

"I have found another cave, young master," was the reply. "Your servant went through the narrow passage at the back of this one and found himself in a cave still larger."

"Another cave!" exclaimed Don eagerly. "Then perhaps there is another outlet through which we can escape."

Abdullah shook his head dejectedly.

"There is no outlet," he said. "I looked for one, but found it not."

"I'm going to take a look at it, anyway," said

Don, rising. "Come along, Brick. Show the way, Abdullah."

They went through a passage barely wide enough to permit their going in Indian file and then found themselves in a cave very similar to the one they had quitted. Don drew his flashlight and scanned the walls carefully, searching every inch of them until he was reluctantly forced to admit that Abdullah's report had been correct. There was no opening that even a mouse could squeeze through.

"Nothing doing," he said disappointedly.

The boys were withdrawing rather dejectedly when Don's flashlight revealed something glittering on the floor. Something curious about it made him stoop and give it a second glance. It was glowing with a greenish, liquid flame.

"What's this?" he exclaimed with a start, as he picked up the tiny object.

A wild thought flashed through his brain, and he looked around, looked to see the floor of the cave studded with coruscating, scintillating points of light.

His voice rose in a shout.

"Emeralds!" he cried. "Uncle Frank! Uncle Amos! Mr. Allison! Alam Bokaru! Come here! We've found the Cave of Emeralds!"

There was a sound of hurrying feet as all the rest of the party, except Alam, who was left on guard, came through the narrow passage, following the sound of Don's voice.

"What? What?" cried the professor.

"Are you sure?" ejaculated the captain.

"At last!" exclaimed Mr. Allison.

"See for yourselves," challenged Don, as he rushed from place to place with Teddy, picking up the glittering jewels. "Here they are! Look at them! Nothing but precious stones ever quiver and flicker like that."

The professor, as the expert of the party, examined them carefully. His hands shook.

"Emeralds!" he pronounced. "Emeralds beyond a doubt, and of the finest quality. We've stumbled on a fortune!"

There was a hubbub of excitement as every one darted here and there, picking up all he could find.

The captain was as deeply stirred as the rest, but he did not forget the foe lurking without.

"Three of us to the front," he commanded. "Come, Don. Come, Mr. Allison. The rest of you gather up what stones there are and stow them away. We've got them now, and, by ginger, we're going to keep them!"

Those who were left behind went over the floor as with a fine tooth comb, until they were sure that none of the tiny stones had been overlooked.

"At least a hundred thousand dollars' worth," estimated the professor. "Possibly double or treble that amount. Enough, in any event, to give each one of us a comfortable little fortune."

"Those Arabs didn't know what a good turn they were doing us when they drove us to seek refuge here," chuckled Brick, as, with Abdullah, he followed the professor into the outer cave.

But there was stern work in prospect, and the finders of the emeralds had to repress their exultation for the present. There would be plenty of time to rejoice over the treasure if they got away from the cave alive.

The afternoon wore on and seemed interminable, especially to Don, whose arm was paining him greatly. The nerves of all were strained to the highest pitch. Not a sound came from without except the complaints and grunting of the camels.

"Alam, how far off do you think those camels are?" asked the captain, about an hour before dark.

Alam listened with practised ears.

"About fifty yards to the right," he answered.

"Do you suppose they are tied?"

"No, master."

The captain took off his cap, put it on the end of his rifle, and poked it out a trifle in front of the cave. No shot followed, though he left it there for several minutes.

"They're not watching the cave," Don observed, as his uncle withdrew the cap. "They're figuring that we won't dare come out."

The captain picked up a bag close at hand and did a little work on some objects it contained.

"Now," he announced, "I'm going outside——"

There was a chorus of protests, which he stilled with a wave of his hand.

"I'm going outside," he repeated. "Keep your rifles ready, though I hope you won't have occasion to use them."

"I'm going along, Uncle Frank!"

"No, Don! You stay right here. There's risk in going out, and if anything should happen you'd be needed by the others."

With this remark, the captain made a way through

the boulders, crouching as low as possible, and dropped noiselessly to the ground.

He lay there a moment, studying the situation. The camels were between him and the bandits and formed an effective shield.

He wormed his way to within fifty feet of the herd. Then he rose and threw a powerful hand bomb in the air so that it would fall to the left of the camels. Two others followed so quickly that all three were in the air at the same time.

Bang! There was a tremendous ear-splitting explosion that filled the grazing beasts with fright.

Bang! Bang! Two other explosions took place at the right, and turned the first fright into uncontrollable panic.

Off the camels rushed, pell-mell, in a mad stampede down the slope. Some of the Arabs rushed to stop them, but had to jump back again to avoid being trodden under the threatening hoofs.

On the beasts went like a rushing torrent, and after them swept the whole crowd of nomads in a frantic effort to recover their mounts. Soon the confused mob of men and brutes utterly disappeared.

"Now's our chance!" cried the captain, as he came running back, while a rousing cheer rose from the party. "It will be dark in a few minutes, and those fellows will be hunting frantically all night to get the brutes rounded up. Out with you now! Bring along your traps, and we'll get on our way!"

Jubilant with delight and excitement at the complete success of the captain's stratagem, the others needed no urging, and with Alam in the lead they took up their journey.

There was to be no resting that night. All the long hours through they hurried along under the unerring guidance of Alam, who could find his way in the dark almost as well as in the daytime. When the dawn came, it found them close to the cave where they had hidden the cars.

To their immense relief, they found the cars just as they had left them.

All were dead tired, but just then no one thought of rest. They got the cars up the slope, the captain, the professor, and Don took their places at the wheels, and with an exulting honk of the horns that might have been interpreted as a last taunting defiance to the enemies they had outwitted, they set out on the long journey to Tuggurt. And not till they had covered a full hundred miles did they stop to rest and sleep the sleep of utter but happy exhaustion.

They made the rest of the journey without obstacle or special incident. At Insalah, Mr. Allison was able to secure some fitting garments, and underwent the ministrations of a barber. Then for the first time they saw him in his proper guise, a tall, handsome, intellectual-looking man of evident breeding and culture.

When they reached Tuggurt, he and Teddy put up at the same hotel as Don and his uncles. There Alam, to whom Mr. Allison felt indebted beyond words for his goodness to his son, was a frequent and welcome guest. Abdullah, too, was made much of because of his fidelity and courage. And in the equitable division of the emeralds that took place, the Arabs received their fitting share, enough in that land of simple needs to make them richer than they had ever dreamed of becoming.

Teddy was deliriously happy.

"Oh, if you could only have the same luck!" he said to Don one night, when all were gathered for a chat in the captain's suite.

"Teddy has told me of the mysterious disappearance of your parents and your sister," said Mr. Allison gently. "I was very sorry to hear of it. But I hope, with him, that you may yet have some news of them. Many times persons are reported to have been lost who have turned up years afterwards."

"I keep on hoping," replied Don, his voice breaking a little, "but it's so long now since the *Mercury* went down——"

"The *Mercury*?" interrupted Mr. Allison quickly. "Was that the name of the ship they were on?"

"Yes," replied Don, his veins thrilling at the question. "Oh, Mr. Allison, you haven't heard— you don't mean——"

"I did hear! I do mean!" cried Mr. Allison, jumping up and beginning to pace the floor in agitation. Why, bless my soul, this is a most singular thing! I met two men who were on the *Mercury* when she met with disaster."

All were now on their feet, pale and shaking.

"Then they weren't all lost?" cried Don, grasping Mr. Allison's arm.

"Bless me, no!" returned Mr. Allison. "Several boatloads got away from the sinking vessel."

"Oh, I'm so glad!" cried Don, sinking into his chair and trying to choke back the sobs that threatened to break from him. Teddy ran to him and put his hand on his shoulder.

"Quick!" exclaimed the captain, pale as death from emotion. "Tell us all you know."

"Yes," urged the professor. "Hurry!"

"Last year," said Mr. Allison, "I met a sailor and a scientist who had been on the *Mercury* on her last voyage. They told me that at least two, and they thought perhaps three, boatloads had time to get away. They did not know what became of the others, as a storm sprang up, and they were separated. But their own boatload was picked up a couple of days later by a sailing vessel and taken to Brazil. The sailor's name I don't know. The scientist was a Professor Webb Reynard, a young Frenchman, I think, by birth, though his English was almost without accent."

"Did he mention the names of any of the others who were among the rescued?" asked Don, his voice trembling.

"No, he didn't," was the reply. "He did say casually that a woman and a young girl were in the boat with him, but that is all."

"What port in Brazil did he say he was carried to?"

"I don't know that he mentioned it. If he did, I've forgotten it."

That was the limit of Mr. Allison's information. But to Don and his uncles it brought renewed hope. Many had escaped. Why might not Don's parents and sister be among them? And the woman and the young girl? Why might not they have been his mother and sister Ruth?

Don could not sleep at all that night, and all through the waking hours from that time on his thoughts were engrossed with the one subject. He would find his parents and Ruth, provided they were alive, if he had to search all over the earth for them.

He had to stay in Algeria until his uncles had fulfilled their mission there. But it was not Africa he saw, as he looked across the sands of the Sahara Desert. In vision, he saw Brazil.

Some weeks later the whole party of Americans reached Havre, and there embarked on a vessel for home.

"Now for God's country!" cried Teddy in glee, when the liner got under way.

"That's the way I've always thought of America," said Don, "but I'll give the name to Brazil, too, if I only find my people there."

The two boys were standing at the rail, but Don's uncles had stretched themselves out in deck chairs.

"The desert has a strange fascination," remarked the captain. "I'm only saying *au revoir* to it, not good-bye. Some day I'm going back there to get to the City of Brass."

"And I to revisit the Cemetery of the Elephants," said the professor. "But with this clue we have to Richard and Alice and Ruth, Brazil, of course, comes first."

"Yes," agreed the captain, knocking the ashes from his pipe, "the desert must wait. Brazil comes first!"

THE END